# CASINO CARTEL

## MICAH REED BOOK 2

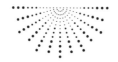

JIM HESKETT

# OFFER

This book was previously published with the title SALLOW CITY.

———————————————————————————————

Want to get the Micah Reed prequel novel **Airbag Scars** for FREE? It's not available for sale **anywhere**. Check out www.jimheskett.com
for this free, full-length thriller.

Also, read on after the main text for some fun, behind-the-scenes extras.

———————————————————————————————

*Gonna talk with the Prince of Peace*
    *Down by the riverside*
    *I ain't gonna study war no more*
    *Study war no more*
    *Ain't gonna study war no more*

— TRADITIONAL

DANNY GARAFFALO SHED his latex gloves and sunk into the chair in the tiny break room at the rear of the morgue. Back aching. He'd been on his feet for nearly three straight hours, bagging and tagging. But that's what happened when they didn't double-check vacation time requests, leaving him the only forensic tech—out of three—in the Genesee County Mortuary for this entire week. He'd always thought late shift would be the slow shift. Not so much.

Danny pondered his half-eaten hoagie, nestled in the waxed paper next to his laptop, and decided his stomach wasn't up to the task of finishing it. Maybe later.

The screen saver sent swirling colors and patterns across his laptop, lulling him into drowsiness. Danny wondered how long he could sit here, letting his unfinished tasks languish until the guilt of laziness would strike him. Those forms weren't going to complete themselves.

Before he could find his answer, the door at the far end of the room opened. Lights bounced off a dozen stainless steel surfaces. Those harsh and buzzing fluorescents. The latch shut with a *clack* and in front of the door now stood a rotund black woman with tidy rows of gray braids clenched to the top of her head. Despite the severe hair, she wore a kind and wrinkly smile, with black eyes like marbles. Looked mid-fifties, maybe. Sixty, tops. She was also wearing a red visitor badge around her neck.

Visitors at this time of night meant someone official. Most families of the deceased came during the day when the medical examiner was present. Danny got to his feet, trying not to grunt from the aches in his back and legs. "Hello."

She stretched, grimacing. "Always think the flight to here from DC is going to be a hop and a skip, but it ends up feeling like I've been pushing a boulder up a hill all day."

"If you flew into Detroit, I can understand. It's hell getting out of that airport. I fly in and out of Bishop when I can."

She grinned, and a rollercoaster of weird silence followed. Obviously, she wasn't here to talk about airport convenience.

"Can I help you, ma'am?"

She dug into her purse and flipped open an ID. Department of Justice. "Are you the medical examiner?"

He eyed the badge. "I'm just a tech, Mrs—"

"Please, call me Anita."

"Well, Anita, the examiner leaves around five most days, or after noon on Friday, if she's had a wet lunch."

Danny felt stupid for saying that, but Anita smiled politely. He cleared his throat. "Is there something I can help you with?"

She put away the ID and adopted a serious face. "I'm with Missing and Unidentified Persons. You have a John Doe I'd like to see."

Danny didn't know if he was supposed to do that, but he supposed a DOJ badge gave her the right to do whatever she wanted. He didn't mind, though, because this Anita woman seemed on the level. Had a kind of folksy air about her. Like someone's grandmother, baking pies and setting tea in the sun to brew.

"You flew from DC to check out a body? We could have sent you the paperwork, if that's what you wanted."

"Thank you, but I would like to see him personally."

Danny's stomach yawned. He suddenly decided he wanted that hoagie, after all. "Sure, Anita, that's no problem. Do you have a reference number?"

She handed him a folded piece of paper with the number on it, and he escorted her to his workstation. He tried to log into the system, but for some reason, she was making him nervous, and he fat-fingered his password a couple of times. Felt a little weird as she watched over his shoulder. Maybe she wasn't technically supposed to see this without a written request, but Danny made the executive decision. If they were going to leave him here alone, that meant he was in charge.

"Got it. He's right over here," Danny said as he pointed at Cold Chamber C. He guided her back through the maze of steel gurneys and opened the door. A fog of wet and frigid steam rushed out, quickly dissolving into the air. "This one's been here a while. We were about to get rid of him. Transfer to a bigger facility."

"I'm here just in time?"

Danny nodded. "You sure are. Chamber D is unusable because of the power outage last month. Capacity issues."

"I understand," she said. "Have the police concluded their investigation?"

"Cops haven't been by yet at all."

She raised an eyebrow. "Is that normal? He's been here for days."

Danny emitted a little chuckle. "You don't know Genesee County."

The body was on top of a steel gurney in the back left of the chamber, wrapped in a white bag. He put a hand on the bag, then paused before rolling it back. "I should warn you, Anita. His face is intact, but the rest of him is... I don't know how else to say it. He's in rough shape. Your John Doe was torn to pieces. Burned, cut, shot, the whole nine yards. I haven't seen too many chewed up this bad before."

Anita smiled her kind and toothy smile. "I've been doing this a long time, dear. I don't think you'll be able to shock me."

He wasn't sure about that. But one way or the other, they would both know in a moment. Danny peeled back the bag over John Doe's face. Tried his best to hide the

8

mass of meat that constituted the body from the neck down. Maybe she could handle it, but *he* didn't want to have to see it again.

He got an eyeful of the charred flesh around the neckline, and he changed his mind about his half-eaten hoagie. Wasn't often that a body could make his stomach squirm.

Anita bent over, her face scrunched up in concentration. Dark eyes flittered over the man's features. The body she was examining was approximately thirty, with brown hair and brown eyes. Caucasian. Good-looking guy, or, at least, he had been before someone had drained the life out of him.

Anita took a business card from her purse and slipped it into Danny's shirt pocket. "If the police do get off their butts and come by to investigate, please call me."

"No problem. I can do that."

She then sighed as she slipped a cellphone from her pocket.

"Bad news?" Danny said.

"Not so much for me, but for someone else, yes. I was really hoping I was wrong about this one." She dialed a number and lifted the phone to her ear. Gave Danny a glance before the call connected. "Frank? It's your little sister… yes, yes, but that's not what I called you for. I'm in Michigan. Flint, exactly. That young man who works for you, what's his name? The one you introduced me to last Christmas."

Danny crossed his arms, intrigued. So this woman had some personal connection to this body. It had seemed strange for someone in the DOJ to come all the way from Washington to identify some random John Doe. But the more Danny thought about it, the more he understood how everything lined up. The way this kid was torn to pieces, it had to be a mafia killing or something like that. Terrorist, maybe. Or perhaps the government themselves had done it. Wouldn't have surprised Danny one bit.

"Right," she said into the phone. "Micah Reed, that was his name. Something caught my eye on a standard MUP search yesterday, and I came out here to Flint to examine it."

She paused, nodding as she listened. Her fingers gripped the edge of the gurney as she pursed her lips.

"That's the thing, Frank. I know this will be hard for you to hear, but I'm staring at Micah's dead body in a morgue right now."

# PART I

## GHOSTS FROM THE PAST

# CHAPTER ONE

F RANK MUELLER SAT up in bed, the light from his phone glazing his legs in an eerie glow. He opened his mouth to speak, but a barrage of coughs came out instead. Damn herbal throat lozenges weren't doing a thing. He hadn't smoked a cigarette in fifteen years, but he still hacked up half his lungs as soon as the sun went down every night.

Just another part of growing old.

When he'd recovered, he managed to spit out, "it can't be Micah's body. It's not possible."

Despite what he'd said, his rational mind told him it was absolutely possible. Every time Micah left the office each evening, Frank knew it might be the last time he'd see the kid alive. Those people from Micah's past were always lurking on the fringes, waiting to rip him to shreds. And Micah dropping out of the WitSec program to fend for himself hadn't been the smartest idea, either.

He heard Anita slide her phone down, and what came out next was muffled. "Do you have any personal effects?"

While Frank waited, he ran through the possibilities. Micah worked for Frank at Mueller Bail Enforcement, but he hadn't been in all week because he was supposed to be on vacation in California. Birthday camping trip. Going to Yellowstone or Yosemite or whatever the hell national park was out there with the big mountains. They hadn't spoken in six or seven days, not since a text message after Micah had landed in Fresno.

Why would he have traveled to Michigan? If he hadn't gone voluntarily, why would someone kill him in California and transport him to Flint? That made no sense at all.

Frank had lived in Michigan, a long time ago. He had no desire to revisit his old stomping grounds.

His phone beeped, and he held it out as a text message came through. A picture of a body, dark blue but somehow pale, with a crinkled body bag peeled back around the head. It was a little hard to tell with all the discoloration of the skin, but that body looked exactly like Micah. Same brown hair and brown eyes. Same chin, same cheekbone structure.

A wave of lightheadedness floated up through Frank.

If that was Micah's body in the morgue, then whoever killed him had done so on behalf of the cartel. That was one thing he knew for sure. Even after disappearing to prison and later emerging into Witness Protection, some of those bastards refused to believe he'd died. Various rumors had circulated. Apparently, not all of them believed the rumors, because the kid had a price on his head.

Someone had come to collect on that bounty. That was a reasonable explanation. Didn't put Frank's ripped heart back to pieces, though.

"Frank? Are you there?"

He cleared his throat and activated the speakerphone so he could run his hands through his thinning hair. He wanted to cry, something he hadn't done in years. "I'm still here, Anita."

"Is that him?"

"I'm not sure," Frank said, even though he was becoming increasingly convinced as he stared at the picture. "It could be."

"I'm sorry you had to find out this way. I thought you might be the one to contact his family."

Most of Micah's family, the McBriars, hadn't seen their son Michael since before he disappeared from public view and then emerged as Micah Reed. They already thought he was dead. That was the best thing for them, because if they discovered he was alive, they'd only put themselves in danger too.

"Let me call you right back," Frank said.

He hung up and looked up Micah's contact record on his phone. His finger hovered over the *call* button, but he couldn't bring himself to press it. Part of him didn't want to know.

Micah had proved himself a capable skip tracer at

Frank's bond agency. And after Micah got sober himself, he'd become a dependable friend.

Frank stood and lumbered to the window. Looked out on his Denver neighborhood, at the aged brick houses, porch lights spitting yellow hues on budding spring lawns. When he'd moved in, he'd been the only black person on this street. The only black cop around. Now, Frank had retired and all the white people were gone, fleeing this grungy neighborhood for the clean and manicured suburbs.

He pressed the button to call Micah.

It rang. And rang. And eventually went to voicemail. Frank hung up, and then he shuffled into the kitchen to refill his water glass. So thirsty, all of a sudden.

He called back and left a voicemail this time. Didn't like the way his voice broke as he spoke into nothingness, sending a message to Micah that the kid might never hear.

Frank walked his phone into the bedroom and slumped on the bed. He let a deep sigh rumble through his body, long enough to make him lightheaded. Then, he called his sister back.

"Which morgue did you say you were at?"

# CHAPTER TWO

MICAH REED STRETCHED his legs out under the seat in front of him, then reached up and tweaked the little nipple to control the airflow. He wondered if the blowing air was being recycled, even though the plane still awaited takeoff. Or, if that weren't true, at what point did they switch it over to inside-only air? When did they lose the ability to touch the outside?

He giggled a little, then realized the people around him probably thought he was crazy. Single white man, alone in an airplane row, laughing at himself. Sure, he could hold his phone up to his ear and pretend he'd been talking to someone, but that might be a little too pathetic.

His body felt heavy, and his brain was full of mush. A week of hiking in California had left him gloriously drained. Had blunted the rollercoaster of thoughts that usually swirled inside his head.

Yesterday, he'd packed up his tent at the Tuolumne Meadows campsite in Yosemite early and decided to spend his last night at a motel nearby. The thought of a night in a nice bed before getting on the plane seemed like a winner. Sleeping in an anonymous bed for his last night of vacation.

The seat next to him was presently empty, but that wouldn't last. Half the plane still had yet to board. While he waited, he took out his phone and powered it on for the first time all week. Seven days without worrying about where he'd left his phone charger. It had been a nice change.

Jettisoning the technology was a close second to his favorite piece of vacation tradition: that relief he felt when he could take his keys and drop them in his bag. No responsibilities for a whole week. No condo key, no car key, no key to Frank's office. Vacation mode.

That had also meant a week without an AA meeting, and he could feel the itch under his skin. The yearning to sit in one of those rooms. He needed to be with his people again, and soon. He didn't feel in imminent danger of taking a drink, but the meetings helped with his general sanity levels. Like a regular oil change for the psyche.

As his phone came to life, a few notifications and messages popped up. Those little numbers in the corners of the apps, screaming *look at me look at me*. Micah hovered his finger over the text message app, but he decided against it. He could afford to remain unplugged for the two-hour flight home, and then deal with civilization after. He flicked his phone into airplane mode and shoved it in his jeans pocket.

As the single-file crowd trickled down the aisle, Micah's jaw almost dropped. One of the hottest women he had seen in recent memory passed the first class curtain, headed into economy class. Hair a shade of red so deep it was almost purple, and green eyes. Arched eyebrows like half moons. Curvy figure under a sharp gray skirt and a button-down shirt, unbuttoned far enough to show a hint of cleavage and the tiny red dots of sparse freckles. Looked early thirties, probably, but Micah was often wrong about that. Within his age bracket, though, for sure.

He glanced at the open seat next to him. Up at the woman. Back at the open seat. No, she wouldn't stop here. Micah's luck wasn't that solid. And what would he say to her even if she did sit next to him? This woman seemed *so* out of his league.

Plus, disposable small talk with people was always a struggle. Couldn't tell them anything genuine about his past, so he usually didn't bother.

Yet, he kept glancing at her and the open seat. She slowed as she neared his aisle. Hefted a roller bag up onto her elbows and flipped it into the overhead storage bin.

Micah's heart vibrated in his chest.

The woman squinted at the seat number on the opposite aisle, then turned back to Micah and slid into the seat next to him.

Welcoming smile that lit up her face like a match in a dark room.

"Hi," she said. "We're going to be neighbors for a few hours."

He cycled through a dozen responses but didn't like any of them. "Looks like it," he said, and immediately felt stupid. A cool guy would have probably shrugged and ignored her because that's what cool guys do.

He seemed to remember being cool once, but that had been a long time ago. Plus, he'd barely spoken to anyone at all for the last week. And that had been the point.

The woman buckled her belt and offered Micah a hand to shake. When she did, her arm pulled the sleeve of her shirt tight, highlighting a muscled shoulder and the pronounced curve of a bicep. Fitness type. Even with the muscles, she still exuded femininity.

"Olivia McDonough." She had a hint of an accent, something eastern but a bit drawl-y, maybe Virginia or Maryland.

"Micah Reed." After hearing her accent, he wondered if his grungy Oklahoma twang had come through. He'd done his best to shed the inflections when he'd moved to Denver.

"Well, Micah Reed," she said, "if you're not the chatty type, let me know. I don't want to bug you if you were planning to plug up your ears with headphones and watch a movie."

He shrugged. "A little conversation wouldn't bother me at all."

Micah noticed she'd pivoted in her seat to face him, and was looking him straight in the eye.

"Business or pleasure?" she said.

"Pleasure. I went on a little vacation for my birthday."

"Oh? Happy birthday."

"Thank you. I spent the last week camping and hiking in Sequoia National Park and then Yosemite. Just me and the trees and the mountains."

She sniffed the air near him and smirked. "You don't smell like you've been camping all week."

He tapped a knowing finger against the side of his nose. "Exactly. That's why I got a motel last night so I could shower this morning."

"Hmm. Smart man."

"What about you, Olivia?"

"I showered last night."

Micah rolled his eyes but still found himself grinning. This woman was quick-witted and a little feisty. He liked that.

"I have some clients in Fresno. Come out here a couple times a year, in the fall and the spring. I don't mind it so much. I usually take a day for myself, drive out to Monterey and lounge on the beach. Anything so I can leave my phone in the glove compartment."

If he hadn't felt so before, now that she'd said the line about ditching her phone, he was positive this woman was a kindred spirit.

"You live in Denver?" he said.

She shook her head. "Got a couple weeks off work, so I'm going to see some friends. Maybe you can point me to some of your favorite spots? Like a good place to get a drink downtown?"

He felt a shade of blush color his cheeks. "I, uh, don't drink."

"Oh," she said, and he could sense her pulling away. Any time he had to tell someone he didn't drink, a little divide popped up. Worse, if they asked him why he didn't drink. Same with telling people he wasn't on social media. He could see they itched to ask why, but he rarely offered anything further. He couldn't tell anyone that if a clear picture of him became public and the wrong people saw it, that would be a death sentence for him, and probably his family, too.

"I can recommend some good places to eat, but I'm afraid I wouldn't know what to tell you about bars in Denver."

After a pause, she said, "No problem. I'm sure I can find out what I need on my own."

# CHAPTER THREE

A N HOUR OR so into the flight, Micah found himself drifting in and out of sleep. The repetitive whir of the plane engines and the constant forward motion made his eyelids weigh as much as boulders. But every time his head lolled forward or to the side, he caught himself and jerked back awake.

Olivia napped in the seat next to him. She looked hot even while sleeping, something most humans couldn't pull off. No snoring, no mouth lolling open with drool making her lip shiny. She slept gracefully, with a tiny hint of a smile on her face as she did. Micah wondered what she might be dreaming about. Those clients of hers in Fresno, probably.

His daydreams about Olivia came to a sudden halt when the plane hit a jolt of turbulence, rattling drinks on trays around him. The seatbelt sign lit up, and a *pong* sound came from above. People murmured as if they'd received a piece of bad news.

Another jolt. Like someone was shaking the plane from the outside. Had put the plane on *vibrate*. The sudden and sharp nature of it unsettled him. The pilot was supposed to warn them of these things.

A few heads poked up above the seats, necks craned around, as if they could find the source of the turbulence. A scratchy voice came from the overhead speakers. "Ladies and gentlemen," it said, and then the rest disappeared as another shake rattled the plane.

A woman at the front of economy class who'd been standing outside the bathroom smacked her head on the folding door, then stumbled down the aisle. "Holy crap," she said, fiercely rubbing her hand against her temple. She wobbled as she tried to find her seat.

A moment later, a man came out of the bathroom, water dripping from his hands and his fly undone. Look of confusion on his face.

Flight attendants dashed down the aisle toward the man, warning him and other standing people to sit and fasten their seat belts. They didn't seem to have the same cool and calm smiles on their faces they usually wore.

Micah glanced at the back of the plane, and one of the flight attendants was talking into a corded phone. Gravely nodding.

Something was wrong here.

The plane rocked and then sank, and Micah's stomach

dropped, that feeling of the beginning of the descent on a roller coaster. Olivia woke up, grasping her stomach.

"What's happening?"

"Turbulence," Micah said.

The plane rocked back and forth, making everything shimmy. A man, two seats over from them, had been watching television on the in-seat screen, but it turned to static.

"I've never felt it so bad before," she said. "This is crazy."

Micah raised the plastic window cover to find the evening sky outside blanketed with charcoal clouds. Several miles away, a bolt of lightning shot through the sky like a knife slashing open black cloth. He reached into his pocket and gripped the severed head of a Boba Fett action figure. He'd been carrying around this little trinket since high school. A gift from his father.

Olivia leaned over Micah's lap, gazing out the window. The scent of her shampoo invaded his nostrils. Something fruity. Despite the rumble of fear in his chest, he felt an overpowering urge to lean in and get a good sniff. Imagined himself running his hands through it, putting a finger under her chin to lift her head and meet her lips with his own.

Another jolt hit the plane, and her head smacked him in the collarbone. She sat back, massaging the top of her head. "Ouch. Sorry about that. Are you sure this is just turbulence?"

He shrugged. "I have no idea what's going on."

The plane dipped again, and Micah's lunch rose from

his stomach into his throat. A few rows ahead, a pair of hands shot into the air, and a phone went flying. A movie or TV show lit up the phone's screen. Micah almost recognized the show, but the phone slammed back down into a different aisle. Objects around the cabin of the plane were like tennis balls on a trampoline. Stationary, then suspended in mid-air for a second.

"What the hell is the problem?" a man from several rows forward said. He stepped into the aisle, and then a burst rocked the plane, and he bent to the side, smacking into the passenger across from him. Micah could hear the *thunk* of their heads colliding. The man stood back up, a dribble of blood now cascading down his forehead. He babbled something about this being unacceptable and then sunk into his seat.

Micah peered out the window again. Another bolt of lightning, this one closer. Now he was starting to feel short of breath. Genuine notion that something was very wrong here. He didn't know if planes were lightning-proof, but it couldn't be good news to be struck by lightning.

The turbulence was now rumbling the plane non-stop. Like sitting in a hyperactive massage chair, shaking everything. Micah's ears and nose itched from the constant jiggling. He pinched Boba's head so tightly he worried he might crush it.

All around him, people chattered and pressed their call buttons, but no flight attendants were rushing out to help. They were probably strapped into their chairs at the back, not willing to risk being tossed at the cabin ceiling.

The captain's voice came on again as the plane took another steep dive, but he was interrupted as the outside filled with light. Bright as day.

At the same moment came the sound of something crashing, as if a car had collided with the plane. The cabin lurched and the outside returned to darkness. Out the window, Micah could see one of the engines and a trail of sparks shooting out from it.

"Oh, shit," he said. "That's definitely not supposed to happen." A few passengers were now shouting, but Micah could barely hear what they were saying over the sounds of the storm. Bursts of white scratched the dark outside. Rain streaked the window, making the outside world a blurry mess.

Olivia reached into the seat back pocket and yanked out the barf bag. Her skin had become tinged with green. "What? What's not supposed to happen?"

"I think we just got hit by lightning."

Micah realized he was strapped in a chair inside a hunk of metal flying through space, and he couldn't do anything to change that fact. Whatever happened after this moment was entirely out of his hands.

Overhead, the plastic panels above the seats popped open, and the air masks dropped down, like the tentacles of a hundred octopi reaching out to caress each passenger.

That's when people started screaming. Every person on the plane writhed and fidgeted in their seats, like one big organism strapped down into flying death chairs. Frantic hands snatched at the oxygen masks.

Micah grabbed the mask and slipped the elastic band over the back of his head. His breath pushed steam into the plastic bag, and his rapid inhalations almost matched the pulse of his heart. He couldn't swallow. Felt like the seatbelt was imprisoning him, and he had an overpowering urge to escape from it and run. But there was nowhere to go.

Olivia clenched his arm. "I don't want to die," she said through her mask. At least, that's what Micah thought she'd said.

He knew he should have probably replied *it's okay, we're going to be fine, when we get through this we'll laugh about it,* but all he said was, "I don't either."

The sparks continued to fly from the engine outside Micah's window. The captain was still speaking, but Micah couldn't hear anything over the screams and shouts of the passengers. Babies crying. The woman in the seat ahead of him was praying, but she lost control of the rosary beads in her hand, and they launched ten rows behind her.

Olivia buried her face in Micah's shoulder. He had a fleeting thought that being in a plane crash was a much better way to get a woman close than watching a horror movie. Guaranteed physical contact. What an odd thing to think at a time like this.

He put his hand on hers, holding her close. She smelled like strawberries, and her skin had a palpable warmth to it. The close contact eased his racing pulse a little, and he tried to normalize his breathing.

She pulled free and looked up at him with frantic eyes.

"I've cheated on my taxes every year for at least the last ten years. I keep expecting them to audit me, but it doesn't ever happen. I don't know why I do it."

So this was confession time. The thought occurred to him to reveal to her that his name wasn't actually Micah, but he couldn't do it. He'd told too many people his secret already.

"That's okay," he said. "Most everybody does."

She smiled and wrapped her arms around his waist. Struck Micah how crazy it was that they were in a plane minus an engine, hurtling toward the earth, and he was so smitten with this woman that being next to her almost made it okay. *Here lies Micah Reed - at the end, he died cuddling with a hot chick, so he had that going for him.*

The bumps from the turbulence came rattling so fast that little objects flew around the plane. A package of pretzels. A plastic cup. In the darkened cabin, people's phones and tablets danced in the air like shooting stars.

He could feel the plane tilting. He leaned forward in his seat, involuntarily. They were headed for the ground. They were going to crash, and there was nothing anyone could do to stop it.

Micah held Olivia tight, and she wept against his shoulder. He peered out the window again, and the sparks had stopped streaking from the engine, but the plane was still diving. Through a break in the clouds, he could see the jagged lines of the mountains west of Denver, some still with late-spring snow capping their peaks.

He'd been excited to see his adopted home again, but not like this.

The descent picked up speed. Micah felt faint as gravity increased. His eyes wanted to shut. His brain ordered him to sleep, pulling him down into blackness. He couldn't hear anything over the roar of the plane, the constant rattling of the tray tables, and the babbling din of the terrified passengers.

Micah closed his eyes and let sleep take him since he didn't think he could resist any longer. As his head lolled forward, the oxygen mask around his face loosened.

And then it stopped.

The plane leveled off, and the roar dimmed back to the normal volume. The ground stayed at an even pace below.

People around Micah started to poke their heads above the seats again. Some laughed. Some clapped. Some shouted about how they were going to sue the airline into bankruptcy. Within ten seconds, talk of a class action suit had already inserted itself into the conversation.

Olivia, who had succumbed to the force of gravity and nodded off, pried open her eyelids and looked up at Micah. "What happened?"

He brushed her hair back from her head. The way she gazed at him, the question in her eyes, made him feel like a protector. Made him feel like he'd done something worthwhile, when all he'd done was not piss his pants.

"It's over."

CHAPTER FOUR

O LIVIA SAT IN Denver International Airport, waiting to return to normal. It hadn't happened yet. Her hands wouldn't stop trembling. She'd been close to death on more than one occasion, but never when she hadn't done something to warrant being in that situation. A bolt of lightning decides to strike in a randomly specific location, and that's it. The plane goes down. Everyone is dead.

Or, the plane almost goes down. She was still alive.

She watched Micah step onto the escalator. When she'd first sat down next to him on the flight, he hadn't seemed cute, but he'd grown on her quickly. That unintentional sort of charm that comes from a lack of sophistication. Not the same kind of unsophistication as a ruddy cowboy in a dive bar might have, but more like the type of guy who doesn't know he's attractive and has no hidden agenda. A refreshing change from the guys she was accustomed to flirting with. The ones who looked at her and saw a collection of pretty holes to violate.

But she also knew how dangerous Micah was.

He turned and gave her one last wink, and she waved back. He held up the little slip of paper on which she'd written her phone number.

It wasn't a real phone number, of course. But it was the only thing she had thought of at the time. She'd had a plan before getting on the flight, and then everything went straight to shit. The plane wasn't supposed to almost crash. That had been a truck-sized wrench in the works. She'd barely been able to speak to Micah at all because of that chaos, and barely able to keep herself together. Hadn't extracted any of the information she'd planned to learn.

Her neck ached from the constant tension of that episode. Admitting the thing about cheating on her taxes had been dumb, but in the heat of the moment, she could have said a lot worse. She could have given away her real purpose for being on that flight.

She stood up from the seat at gate 43 and ran a hand through her hair to pull it back into a ponytail. Across the building at gate 44, a little girl was standing below her mother, trying to reach up and take the mother's phone from her hands. The toddler couldn't have been more than three years old. At that age, so helpless against the world. The mother swatted at those tiny hands, and the girl pouted. Stuck out her lower lip and crossed her arms. She stopped short of stomping her feet, but that would probably come next.

Olivia felt her food swimming in her stomach. She'd only not thrown up through some miracle. Divine intervention, or something like that. If only she had the time to seek out a five-star masseuse in Denver and indulge in a couple of hours of recuperation. It might take someone that long just to work the knots out of her shoulders.

The phone in her purse vibrated, and she dug it out.

"I just heard about the flight," a male voice said. "Are you okay?"

She used her free hand to pinch her shoulder as she sauntered back toward the terminal. Glanced back at the mother and daughter. The mother had given the phone to the child eventually, of course.

"Olivia?"

The urgency and worry in his voice annoyed her, but she didn't know why. "It's fine, Jeremy. No one was injured, and the plane landed without any problems. NTSB was here, running around like chickens with their heads cut off. They got my info for a follow-up interview."

He mumbled something about keeping a low profile, but she couldn't hear him clearly.

"Apparently," she said, "planes don't need all of the engines, which makes me wonder why they bother having all of them in the first place. Where are you?"

"I'm at the waiting area parking lot. I can be at the baggage claim in ten minutes."

"Okay, I'm walking that way now."

Jeremy paused. "Well?"

"Yes, he was on the flight. Micah Reed is not the John Doe in the Flint morgue."

CHAPTER FIVE

MICAH STOOD IN the parking garage below his downtown Denver condo, staring at the voicemail notification his phone was practically begging him to check. The little red *2* in the corner of the app looked terribly sad. *Press me press me press me.*

At one point during his camping trip in Yosemite, as he stood on a hiking trail that faced the vast Half Dome rock, he paused to sip from his Nalgene and catch his breath. At that moment, awed by the sheer scope of nature, he decided to give up technology. Then, he remembered television and video games and having all the content of the world at the touch of a button. Hard to give that up.

So Micah tapped the phone app to check his voicemail and begin his return to the real world. The message started playing, and his mouth immediately dropped open. He was listening to a scattered and urgent voicemail from Frank, his boss and AA sponsor.

"Micah, if you get this, I don't know what to do," Frank said. His tone was harsh, near crying. "I'm in a morgue in Flint, staring at a John Doe who is like a carbon copy of you. But it can't be you because you're in California, right? I was trying to remember if you had a birthmark or scar or something, but I don't know any of that crap. Please call me as soon as you get this."

A body in a morgue?

Micah let the phone drift from his ear. Felt a little chill run up his spine. Going from the rollercoaster of almost dying in a near-plane crash, to getting Olivia's phone number, to this, he didn't know what to think. He sat on the floor of the parking garage, next to his car.

Then he dialed Frank.

"Oh, Lord," Frank said as soon as the call connected. "I knew you were still alive."

"I just got back to my place and listened to your message. I don't understand what's going on here."

"My sister works for the DOJ, in Missing and Unidentified Persons. You remember Anita, right?"

"Sure. Last Christmas. She bought me socks."

Frank paused to cough. "She was doing random screenings and came across a body in Michigan tagged as John Doe. This person looks just like you, Micah. It's eerie. Same hair and eyes and nose and everything."

The shock began to dissipate as Micah put some of the pieces together. Halfway across the country, a body had turned up in the morgue that looked exactly like him. A dead person. A John Doe. Someone had killed this nameless person, and it seemed unlikely it could be a coincidence that this person looked exactly like Micah.

Could it be a coincidence?

Something told Micah it wasn't But, if so, what did it mean?

The parking garage door opened and in strode a family of four. Two women holding hands, two small children tottering along behind them. The kids struggled to keep up with the grownups, who were practically jogging to a car. Micah didn't recognize them. It was a big building with probably hundreds of residents Micah had never seen before.

And there were hundreds of buildings in Denver just like this one. Thousands of cities across the world, and billions of people. But no two people were the same.

An itch of an idea occurred to him. "Are you at the morgue right now?"

"No. I'm at a motel nearby."

"Do you think you'd be able to tell if he'd had plastic surgery?"

"I know where you're going with this. Now that I know it's not you, that's the only possibility that makes any sense. Unless you have a twin brother that I don't know about."

"I have a brother, but he's not my twin."

Micah watched the family hop into the car and peel out of their parking spot. "I want to see the body. I can be on a flight to Detroit in a couple hours. Tomorrow morning, at the latest. If they did this, Frank, I need to know about it."

"I know who you're talking about when you say 'they,' and I don't think that's a good idea."

"Why?"

"Alright, kid, I'll spell it out for you. Because, if someone killed a lookalike of you for something related to Velasquez's Sinaloa cartel—to collect a price on your head or something like that—what do you think they'll do if you show up in person and start digging around? You think the cartel or whoever did this would be happy to see you?"

Micah chewed on his lower lip, ran through some possible rebuttals, but couldn't come up with anything that didn't sound whiny. Frank was right.

"It's best if you stay in Denver. Sit this one out. Besides, someone should be at the office in case any work comes in."

"I get it, Frank."

"I'll run over to the morgue and give you a call after. Check out marks for plastic surgery."

"Text me a picture."

Frank hesitated. "I'm not sure what good that will do. It's like staring at a mirror image of you, but he's all mangled and destroyed. It's disturbing. One of the worst I've ever seen. Are you positive you want to see that?"

"No, I guess not," Micah said. They gave their goodbyes and Micah hung up. Stared at the empty spot where the family's car had been. A little puddle of oil on the concrete.

Then he checked his phone to find the next flight to Michigan.

# CHAPTER SIX

OLIVIA AND JEREMY sat in the rental car on 15th, gazing up at Micah's condo building. Denver's Cherry Creek rushed next to the street, with the massive REI building in the old train station across from that. This part of downtown seemed half brand new skyscraper condos comprised of glass and steel, and half aging buildings preserved in time.

Olivia's neck still pulsed from the tension of the flight fiasco. There wasn't enough Ibuprofen in the world to return it to normal, and every tilt of her head reminded her of the pain. She still hadn't made time to see a masseuse.

"He's probably not home," Jeremy said.

She traced a finger along her right eyebrow, smoothing it. "Doesn't matter one way or the other. If he *is* inside, don't let your guard down for a second. Micah Reed is a cold-blooded killer, and he'll be on his home turf."

Jeremy sucked on his teeth. "Should we wait to be sure?"

"No. If he's gone, we poke around and see what we can find. If he's here, then we'll deal with him. It's going to happen at some point."

He smiled at her from the passenger seat, then reached across and laid a palm on the back of her hand. She stared down at his hairy hand flesh.

"Do you want to talk about the flight? I'm sure it was scary."

She slipped her hand out from underneath his. So relentless with these questions about the stupid flight. "No. I don't want to talk about it. It happened, so whatever. We didn't die. The plane landed. I'm sure I can find a way to join a class action to sue the crap out of the airline, so I can, at least, find a silver lining there. If I wanted to."

"I just thought…"

"Not now, Jeremy."

He ducked his head like a shamed dog. She hated when he did that. He would pout, and make her feel guilty, and then she'd find herself apologizing by taking her clothes off in his hotel room later. And that was a habit she needed to break. She was supposed to be his boss, after all.

"I'm sorry," she said, and then she pointed up at the condo building. "Can we just deal with this first, and then we'll talk about that later?"

"Sure, sure. You want me to bring the laptop?"

"Might come in handy."

He popped open the briefcase on the floor and removed

a 9mm, then screwed a noise suppressor onto the barrel. He slipped a laptop into a messenger bag and slung it over his shoulder. "I'm ready if you are."

Olivia checked the magazine in her pistol and shoved it into a pocket inside her jacket. If she had to kill Micah, she wondered if she might feel a moment of hesitation since she'd experienced a genuine connection yesterday. She'd never had to eliminate anyone for whom she'd felt anything above contempt.

A moment of hesitation might be all he needed.

She nodded at Jeremy, and they left the car to cross the street. The condo had a lobby and what looked like a desk for a doorman or receptionist, but no one stood behind it now. She tilted her head at the elevators and Jeremy followed. The lobby smelled of fresh flowers, but she didn't see any around. In a nice building like this, they probably pumped it straight through the air vents.

"Should we access the garage and find out if he's home first, so we can be sure?" Jeremy said.

Olivia considered it. "No, because if we check it out, go upstairs and have to take him out, all we've done is increase the chance that we might leave a witness."

"Good point. I didn't think of that."

They stepped into the elevator and hit a snag when they found a keycard access swipe to activate the floor buttons.

He sighed. "Shit. We should have anticipated this."

"Stairs will probably have one too."

"We could wait for someone to come along, but that

puts us in the same position as going into the parking garage."

Olivia opened the panel next to the buttons and squinted at the bank of electronics and wires inside. Since there wasn't an obvious *disconnect card swipe* button, she puzzled over how to proceed. But she did have one idea.

"I got this," she said. She took out her pistol and flipped it, so she was gripping the barrel in one hand.

"What are you doing?"

"I already told you, I got this," Olivia said as she smacked the panel with the butt of the pistol. *Whack whack whack.*

It cried and bent, but didn't engage, so she whacked it again.

*Beep.*

Lights came on from behind the panel, which was now dented enough to see inside. She pressed the elevator button and it started moving. A desire to laugh bubbled up inside her, because who the hell would think something like that could actually work? "Just like my mom fixing the TV when I was a little kid."

Jeremy shook his head as the elevator soared through space toward Micah's floor. "That kind of stuff is going to get us caught. Small footprint, remember?"

She shrugged, even though he was right. "Getting into Micah Reed's apartment is all I care about right now. No one saw us, so anything else is secondary."

The elevator door opened, and they emerged out onto

lush white carpet. She could feel her flats sink into it on the first step.

"This is fancy," Jeremy said, dragging a toe across the carpet like running a hand through tall grass. Original canvas art hung from the walls, ornate brass sconces at intervals. Didn't seem like the kind of place Micah would live. Given what she knew of him, at least. Money couldn't buy class, no matter how hard it tried.

"El Lobo paid well," Olivia said. "Even for snitches like Michael McBriar, or Micah Reed, or whoever he thinks he is."

They stopped outside the door and readied their weapons.

Jeremy took out a couple of small lockpick tools and bent to examine the lock. "He'll hear this if I can't get it unlocked quick enough."

She hunkered down a bit, gun at a slight angle. "That's fine. I'm good to go."

Jeremy picked the lock to open the condo door. A dark room greeted them, no traps or bullets flying through the air.

The decor inside matched the carpet outside. Vaulted ceilings, stainless steel appliances, clean paint on the walls. Not much in the way of personal touches, few paintings and pictures on the walls. Stark, like a first college apartment, except for a lack of marijuana leaf posters.

But no Micah. No attack dog or mewling cat, either.

Jeremy padded through the living room, his gun pointed at the floor. He ducked into one room, then another, then into the bathroom. He turned back to her and shook his head. "It's clear."

"Okay," she said. "So, he's not here. Now that we're in, let's learn what we can and get out quick. I'd rather not have him surprise us while we're here."

Olivia and Jeremy split up, and she first checked the kitchen, looking in standard hiding spots, such as under the drawers, behind the oven, inside containers in the freezer.

Nothing.

"Got anything back there?" she called to him.

"There's some wear on the carpet back here in the bedroom. Scratches on the baseboards. It's worth a look."

She passed a spare bedroom filled with guitars, and then joined Jeremy in the master bedroom. He was picking at a section of the carpet against the back wall that looked as if it had been repeatedly lifted.

She knelt and pulled up the carpet, then jiggled the floorboards underneath to reveal a hiding space. Shoebox sitting in the dark below.

"Jackpot," she said.

Jeremy lifted the shoebox and opened it. Inside, they found some letters, all of them old. High school, looked like. Plus some pictures, and then two flash drives. She lifted one picture of Micah, taken at least a few years ago, standing with the man referred to in Michael McBriar's files as his best friend, now deceased. This young man's arm was draped over Micah's shoulder, both of them wearing wide grins. Looking either drunk or blissfully happy.

She thought of the flight, how easily she'd clung to Micah's arm, practically folded into him when she was so deep in her panic. And even though she'd known what Micah Reed was capable of, she hadn't thought twice about it at the time.

"What's that?" Jeremy said.

"Pug."

He cocked his head. "Huh?"

"Real name Philip Gillespie, but he went by Pug. He was also a member of the Sinaloa, and Micah's running buddy. He died sometime after the feds initially contacted Micah, but before the trial."

She dropped the picture back into the pile to keep searching. Below the pictures, she found a business card with a raised image of a wolf's head. Olivia already knew what that card meant. The Sinaloa cartel gave out very few of these cards, so how had Micah gotten one?

She had an urge to stash it in her pocket.

"WitSec wouldn't have allowed him to keep all this," Jeremy said. "It's too damaging."

"Exactly. He had to smuggle this, somehow." She pointed at the flash drives. "Copy those."

He opened his laptop and jammed in the first flash drive, then started copying over the data. "Are we taking the shoebox?"

She shook her head. "If we can get in and out before he comes home, I'd rather him not know we were ever here."

Jeremy finished copying the first flash drive and plugged in the second.

"Anything useful?" she said.

He flicked along the laptop trackpad. "Music, looks like, on the first thumb drive. Couple hundred files here. This second one has some spreadsheets, but they don't make any sense. There are no labels."

He spun the laptop around and pointed it at her. All she could see were cells filled with numbers, but no guide to explain what they meant.

"It may mean nothing, but it's probably worthwhile to have it anyway."

Jeremy angled his head around, taking in Micah's sparse bedroom. "Think he's on his way to Michigan?"

"Probably."

"So that's where we're going next?"

After he finished copying the second flash drive and handed it back to Olivia, she returned everything to the shoebox and replaced it under the floorboards.

"We're not going to Michigan yet. There's another acquaintance of Micah's here in Denver we need to see."

# CHAPTER SEVEN

MICAH STOOD IN the security line at Denver International, slowly inching toward the TSA checkpoint. Despite the enormity of the terminal, he felt claustrophobic. He watched the faces of all the other sullen people weaving through the snake-like line, getting ready to slip off their shoes and scramble through bags to remove laptops.

The slip of paper with Olivia's phone number weighted down his pocket. He hadn't found a good time to call her, and he might not find one for a few days, not with everything potentially involved in this trip.

Another trip on an airplane.

An airplane to Michigan to visit a dead body with his face.

His same face.

While Micah didn't know who had done this, he had a strong suspicion of *why* they had done this. And it brought up all manner of disturbing side effects. Repercussions that could extend not only to Micah but to his family and any friends he might still have out there.

Not that he knew if he had any friends left from his old life, since he hadn't spoken to any of them in years.

He slogged through the line, and his thoughts kept flashing back to last night, to a dream he'd had. It was only a twinkling of memory now. Something about being in a chair, not able to stand up, even though he desperately wanted to escape the chair and rise to his feet. Like a burning compulsion. In the dream, he'd had trouble opening his eyes, and he wondered if his waking self had been trying to open his eyes to flee the dream.

He'd woken in a puddle of sweat, with a feeling that something in his bedroom was different. Or something in the condo. Wearing only his underwear, he walked from room to room, checking for anything out of the ordinary. He even took the shoebox out of the hiding spot under the baseboards but found nothing out of place. His pictures, letters, flash drives. A rare picture of him and his best friend, at the Bricktown Canal in Oklahoma City, and one of them in Canyonlands National Park.

Nothing had been disturbed.

Eventually, he'd chalked it up to after-effects of the nightmare, which had already started to fade.

Now, with each step toward that TSA checkpoint, he came closer to boarding another airplane. Another chance to put his life in the hands of someone else. His mouth was as dry as his armpits were wet. Wished he'd brought a bottle of water with him. His heart had turned into a rattling snare drum at the mere thought of strapping himself into that seatbelt.

Plenty of people who'd stepped off the plane from Fresno had talked about suing the airline. Micah had no interest in joining that insanity. He wanted to put those thoughts behind him, nightmares or no.

Besides, he couldn't have two near-crashes in the same week, could he? That didn't seem possible.

He stepped up to the front of the TSA line and handed his license and boarding pass to an inattentive woman standing behind the podium. She flashed a miniature blacklight over the license and flickered her eyes at him. The license wouldn't raise any flags since the federal government had issued it to a man named Michael McBriar, who then immediately became Micah Reed. It was as genuine as anyone else's in the TSA line.

"Any liquids over three ounces?" she said.

Micah shook his head.

She eyed him, gave a dramatic pause, and then scribbled a circle around the destination on his boarding pass.

Flint, Michigan. Then, the morgue, where a dead body waited for him.

## CHAPTER EIGHT

OLIVIA PARKED THE car a half a block down the street from the Pink Door strip club and killed the engine.

Jeremy pointed to the gun range across the street. "Shooting over here, boobs over there. Classy neighborhood."

"We're not here to take in the local culture."

"Denver acts like it's such a whitewashed and hip place, but it has crime and ghettos just like every other big city in the world. I hate this town."

"I suppose it's not New York or Paris, but I don't mind it. What's gotten into you?"

He leaned back against the headrest. "We still haven't had that conversation you promised me."

"Soon, Jeremy. Can we please stay focused for right now?"

He popped the glove box and retrieved his pistol, then

took out a noise suppressor from his jacket pocket. "If that's the way you want it. We going in strapped?"

"You better believe it," she said.

They left the car and approached the strip club. Her shoes splashed in tiny puddles from a spring rain. A neon sign over the club's door blasted her eyeballs, and cast a wide aura of tawdriness. The door to the strip club was literally pink.

A muted *whump whump* of bass reverberated through the walls of the building and out into the street. Inside the club, they paid the admission price and crossed into the blacklight-tinged glow of the main room. Dancers on poles, alluring waitresses hustling drinks, lonely men thrusting dollar bills at g-strings. Teeth glowing white from the light.

Olivia hadn't been to one of these places since college, for a friend's bachelor party. Not her kind of scene, with the dancers throwing themselves at her, pretending to be as attracted to her as they did with the men. She knew even then it was just a marketing strategy. If the dancers appeared to be bisexual, they doubled their potential customer base. Simple math.

Olivia snapped her fingers in front of Jeremy's face since he'd become eye-locked with a stripper across the room who looked roughly eighteen years old. He gave Olivia a sheepish grin.

If she slept with him tonight, he'd be thinking of that baby-faced stripper, and Olivia didn't like that. Didn't like competing for attention.

She flashed her eyes to a table at the back of the room, lights hanging low to obscure the faces of the men seated around it. Two bouncers stood nearby the table, further obscuring the occupants.

Definitely where they needed to be.

She unbuttoned the top button of her shirt, allowing a hint of cleavage to poke through. Then she strutted toward that table as if she had every right to be there. She threw her sex out in front of her like a lasso, because she knew from experience that even trained soldiers would overlook the most lethal woman when they had a pair of tits shoved in their faces.

Jeremy tottered behind like a puppy. That was just as well, because if he appeared to be subordinate, he wouldn't seem threatening.

As she approached the table, the two bouncers slinked closer together, blocking her view. Tits or no, they weren't going to let her stride up to that table. They guarded him like a government asset, when Olivia already knew this man was far from legit.

And she'd already seen him; the chubby man at the table with the banana-shaped scar underneath one eye. She heard him bark something, and the bouncers parted. Grin on his face a mile wide, and that lustful look in his eyes. He waved her forward.

"Hi," he said, nearly shouting over the music. "I'm Tyson. Welcome to my club."

She sat at the table and tried to take stock of the two men on either side of Tyson. They were wearing sports coats, and she couldn't see a gun bulge from shoulder holsters on either, but she had to assume they were packing. Because of the vents in the back of their blazers, they wouldn't have pistols in their waistbands. Too awkward to draw quickly. No, had to be wearing armpit holsters. She would need to watch for any cross-body movements.

"I know who you are, Mr. Darby. I'm a big fan of your business."

He tilted his head and picked at a plate of french fries on the table. He had equal piles of ketchup and mayonnaise for dipping. "Are you? You like the adult entertainment industry? Or is it my lawnmower repair shop you're referring to?"

"Neither."

His smile faltered a bit, and then he flicked his head at Jeremy. "That guy with you?"

Jeremy was still outside of the bouncer wall beyond the table. "Yes," she said. "He's just here to make sure I don't get into any trouble, which I sometimes do in these places." She could tell from his expression that he liked this kind of innuendo, and she filed that away in case she needed to use it later. Men are such simple creatures. Sex, violence, approval. Some combination of the three would earn their heart every time.

"What kind of trouble would you get into?"

She shrugged. "The night is young, so we'll see. In the meantime, we can talk business."

"Are you a cop?"

She shook her head. "Like I said, just a fan."

"Well, then," Tyson said. "What can I do for you? Are you interested in applying for a job?" His eyes drifted to her cleavage. "You appear to be qualified, and I am in fact looking for a new girl right now."

"I appreciate the vote of confidence, but I'm not here on a job search. I want to talk to you about Micah Reed."

His expression dimmed as she could see him process the information. A spark of recognition lit up his eyes, and then his face darkened further. He was bordering on a scowl. "I might know who that is."

"What's your relationship with him?"

"Why should I tell you that?"

"Because I work for some people who are interested in knowing more about him. That's all."

Tyson sat back and tugged at the wiry goatee sprouting from his chin. She scooted her chair closer to the table and slipped a hand into her purse without breaking eye contact. Tyson and the men on either side of him hadn't seemed to have noticed, since she kept it all under the table.

"Micah Reed visited my establishment not too long ago," Tyson said. "He walked around, stared at the girls, and didn't order anything to drink. Didn't spend a dime. I don't trust people who don't drink, so I asked him to leave. That's all I'm willing to say about it."

Olivia was taken aback and had to close her eyes for a second to compose herself. "He doesn't work for you?"

"No, he does not."

Could Tyson be lying about this? She didn't like having bad information.

While she was considering this new angle, Tyson's eyes snapped to the bouncers beyond the table, and Olivia slipped the gun from her purse.

"I'm not sure I'm interested in talking to you more about anything," Tyson said. "It's time for you to tell me who you work for. New York? Chicago? If someone important in Denver employed you, I would have known about you. I know everyone in this town."

Olivia narrowed her eyes. "My employers are my business, so we're not going to discuss that."

Tyson leaned a little closer and popped a french fry in his mouth. "What you want to tell me and what you *will* tell me are very different things. Maybe you think you can just get up and walk away, but now you've piqued my interest. Flashing your tits and batting your eyes. You think I'm some horny teenager? Underestimating me is a big mistake, sweetheart."

She wrapped her finger around the trigger. "Mr. Darby, I've got a 9mm with a noise suppressor pointed right at your crotch. With this loud music, I can squeeze off half a dozen shots before anyone even notices."

The guards on either side of Tyson slipped hands into their jacket pockets and confirmed her suspicions. Armpit holsters.

"Is that so?" Tyson said, grinning. "My men here will notice. Between you and any door to the outside, you'll find ten men with semi-automatic weapons ready to cut you into pieces. You can try batting your eyes at them, but they'll kill you anyway."

Olivia couldn't see Jeremy, but she had to hope he'd been following the conversation well enough to have drawn his weapon. If not, she probably wouldn't make it out of this club alive. "That may be true, but I'll shoot both of your balls off before they can do anything to stop me."

Tyson paused, then clapped his hands together and laughed. Wiped a smear of mayonnaise off his lip.

She hesitated. Didn't know what to make of this guy.

"Okay, little lady, there's no need for that. You don't have to tell me who you work for. I have a pretty good idea already. But tell me one thing: why are you so interested in Micah Reed?"

Some of the tension rolled out of her shoulders as she released her grip on the trigger. Pursed her lips. She considered how to phrase her answer to Tyson's question.

"Because," she said, "there are some open loops that need to be closed."

# CHAPTER NINE

**M**ICAH STEPPED OFF the jetway and lumbered into the Bishop Airport in Flint. Felt the difference in humidity immediately as he drew in his first breath of local air. He had to push and pull just a fraction harder to work his lungs.

As he entered the building, he glanced back at the airplane, hooked to the jetway. A giant steel torpedo that soared through the air, hundreds of miles per hour. No sudden bolts of lightning. No oxygen masks descending from above. No screaming passengers preparing for death with prayers or curses. No major turbulence, although his heart had been racing the whole time, waiting for it.

Halfway through the flight, his jaw ached from the constant tension. His jeans wore dark patches of sweat from where his hands had been gripping his thighs. The lady sitting next to him kept tossing looks, frowning at him.

But that was over now. He was in Flint, on the ground, alive.

The whole of the airport possessed half a dozen gates. The interior was steeped in gray tones as if someone had put a filter on everything. As he wandered toward the baggage claim, hunting for the car rental desks, Frank appeared from behind a sunglasses kiosk next to the business center. Arms crossed, a scowl on his face.

Micah waved. "Hey, Frank. How did you know?"

"I was a cop, or did you forget? I could hear it in your voice that you were going to do the most stupid thing possible and hop on a plane out here."

Micah hitched his backpack higher on his shoulder. He wasn't terribly surprised, since Frank knew him better than most people. He could have even predicted the angle of the scowl on Frank's face.

Micah wondered if Frank could see the patches of palm sweat on his jeans. Could detect the lingering hangover of tension on his face. "I'm here now. I want to help."

Frank chewed his lip but did not respond.

Micah watched people walking to and from gates. He never knew how to judge a city by the content of its airport people. They could be from anywhere.

"Yes, you're here now," Frank said. "So, let's get out of this public space before anything strange happens."

They walked along the path of the terminal, toward the exit. "This is your town, right? You lived here."

"A little closer to Detroit, actually, but I know the Flint area. Spent some of my best cop years here and in some of these nearby towns." Frank held up a flat hand and pointed on his palm, below his thumb. "We're here, on the hand. Do you know about the hand? Some people call it the mitten."

Mitten?

Micah thought about it for a second, and then the answer seemed obvious. "Mitten. Because of how Michigan is shaped?"

"You got it."

"That's clever. I can't wait to learn all about the state lore from a local. We'll take selfies together at all the sights."

Frank scowled. "This isn't funny, kid. If you're going to stay here, you'll need to shave your head and grow a mustache or something."

"Shaving the head I can do, but the mustache… not so much. That's my one-sixteenth Cherokee blood curse. We don't do facial hair so good. But I suppose that's what I get for being born in Oklahoma, of all the dumb luck. I don't remember anyone giving me a choice in the matter."

Frank didn't seem to be in the mood for witty banter. He waved Micah toward the airport exit, and Micah followed, navigating through the crowd of commuters with their pressed suits and roller bags. When they stepped outside, the humidity kicked it up a notch. Like walking through a damp curtain.

"Then we're going to get you some fake prescription glasses," Frank said as he pointed to a rental car parked in short term parking.

As they slid into the car, Frank said, "happy birthday, by the way."

"Thank you."

"Was it a good one, your trip?"

"Yeah. I spent my actual birthday in the Tuolumne area of Yosemite, hiking around some lakes there. Hardly saw any people on that side of the park. It was wonderful."

"Bears?"

Micah shrugged. "Saw a few. None that came close or bothered me."

Frank put his hand on the key in the ignition. "That's good. I'm always worried about bears whenever I leave the city.

"But that's what makes it fun."

Frank sighed and shook his head. "You shouldn't have come, kid."

# PART II

IF YOU SEEK A PLEASANT PENINSULA

# CHAPTER TEN

**M**ICAH STOOD IN front of the mirror in the motel room bathroom, barely able to recognize himself. A few tiny patches of stubble that he'd missed with the razor were all that remained of his hair. The black-rimmed fake prescription glasses he was wearing veiled his eyes, but even those didn't look the same. Blue contact lenses masked his normally brown eyes.

He wasn't the same person. Not Micah Reed. Not Michael McBriar, who he used to be before all this mess with the cartel and the trial. He was someone new, someone nameless.

He stared at the head of Boba Fett, sitting on the soap tray underneath the mirror. Boba didn't recognize him anymore. But the little space bounty hunter would forgive him, as always. Boba was like that.

"Is your sister still here?" Micah called out.

"What?"

"Anita. Is she still in town?"

In the main part of the motel room, Frank switched on the TV. "She went back to DC this morning. She can maybe come back later in the week, but she has meetings she can't miss. Wheeling and dealing and all that."

Micah left the bathroom and joined his boss/AA sponsor. They had opposing double beds in their cheap motel room, covered with floral print bedspreads. "Big trees here."

"Trees where?"

"The trees here, in Michigan. They're massive, like big green knives trying to stab the sky."

"You noticed those trees right away, did you?"

"I sure did. It's what makes me a great skip tracer. My attention to detail."

Micah ran a hand over the hairless surface of his head. His fingers traced a cool line against his skin. The shape felt weird, not quite round, as he would have expected.

Frank hit mute on the TV remote. "Something on your mind?"

"I met a woman on the plane. Not my flight here, but the flight from Fresno to Denver. Flat-out gorgeous, as in, way out of my league. Red hair, green eyes, named Olivia. A year or so ago, I wouldn't have even been able to say three coherent words to her. But I had a moment of clarity and managed to snag her phone number."

"You going to call her?"

Micah thought about it. "It'll have to wait. I don't know if I want to tell her I'm in Michigan, looking into a dead body that has my face. Might be a little too personal up front. We were on the plane together. I mean, when all that trouble happened."

"You've barely said a word about it. Maybe it's time we talked it through. You know, how you're doing with it now and all that."

Micah sat on the bed opposite Frank's, not liking how far down he sank when he put his full weight on it. Too soft beds equaled a bad night's sleep. "It was wild. Terrifying, exhilarating, draining. I don't know how else to describe it. I guess I didn't think we were going to die, but I wasn't as scared as I maybe should have been."

"Did it make you want to drink?"

"That's the thing, Frank. I didn't experience any cravings at all. I don't think taking a drink popped into my head once during that insanity."

Frank scratched fingernails through his gray hair. "You've been sober seven months now, right?"

Micah didn't have to do the math. His sobriety date was etched into his brain, along with the daily count since his last drink. Two hundred and seven days since he'd woken from a blackout near downtown Denver, the last time he'd swallowed any alcohol. "Yes, give or take."

"Living a sober life means a lot more than not drinking. It bleeds into everything you do, just like the drinking bleeds over into everything. You can't... ahh, what's the word? *Segment*. You can't segment your life into buckets. It's all one big stew, basically."

"So I'm getting better at handling real-life stuff because of sobriety?"

Frank nodded. "Alcohol is fading as your go-to stress reliever. You've probably heard people in meetings talking about handling life on life's terms. And if you keep working the steps, it'll keep getting better."

"Life getting better sounds right up my alley," Micah said.

"Tell me what the first step says."

"Admitted that I'm powerless over alcohol and that my life is unmanageable."

"You should be learning that it's not just alcohol," Frank said. "Life itself is out of your control, and you're power-less over everything."

Micah shook his head. "That doesn't register. I mean, I have power over some things. How can I be powerless over everything? I refuse to believe that my fate is predestined."

"That's not what I'm saying."

Micah adjusted his glasses. Having the extra weight on his face would take some getting used to. "Then I don't understand."

"Give it time. You'll get it."

"If you say so. I would like to hit an AA meeting as soon as possible. Getting a bit restless."

"No problem, kid. I know of one nearby." Frank switched off the TV and looked Micah in the eye. "Let's talk about how we're going to handle investigating this John Doe."

Goosebumps dotted Micah's forearms. "Okay."

"Here's something to think about. If your theory is true, and whoever killed this poor guy did it to make the cartel think you're dead, then maybe we should leave it that way."

"What are you saying, Frank?"

"The government spread rumors you'd died, after the trial. But, as we've heard, not everyone in your old organization believed those rumors."

"Right," Micah said. "I mean, obviously, they don't, because there's still a price on my head. Which is probably why that poor guy is lying in the morgue. But if you're saying we don't try to find out what happened… what about justice for this dead person?"

Frank paused. "Is that what you want? Even though involving the cops and proving this man isn't you puts you back at risk?"

The weight of the dilemma hit Micah. A chance to walk away, make the cartel—once and for all—think he was dead. He'd still have to live somewhere under his assumed name, still have to stay off social media, but he wouldn't be actively hunted any longer.

A chance to be free. To a certain extent.

But it came at the expense of letting this dead man continue to impersonate him. If this John Doe had a family, they would never know what had happened to him. He would always be another missing person, with no body ever to turn up. No closure for anyone and everyone who had ever noticed that he'd gone missing.

"I don't know. What if we don't involve the cops yet and we investigate on our own?"

Frank let loose a barrage of coughs that culminated in a wet gurgle. "That's an option."

"Then I think we have to find out his identity. It's the right thing to do."

"Okay," Frank said. "But no cops means no fingerprinting, no DNA."

"Wait a second. He was murdered, right? Wouldn't the cops be investigating it already?"

Frank shook his head. "I thought you might want to go down this path, so I asked Anita to put a stop to that. Local PD hadn't done anything yet, anyway, so it was easy for her to handle."

"How does that work?"

"She'll make it a federal matter, and the paperwork will get shuffled around for a few days to keep it in limbo. This case is completely at our discretion. If we do nothing, he goes to a pauper's grave in Genesee County."

Micah thought about the body rotting in the ground, no one ever knowing who he was. Unacceptable. "Can Anita use her resources to identify him?"

Frank frowned. "Not really, now that she's keeping it under the rug. We have three or four days, tops, in order to gather info without anyone noticing. After that, she'll have to turn it over to someone, unless we can give her a good reason not to."

"And we're on our own."

"It's going to be old school," Frank said. "You know, knocking-on-doors kind of detective work to figure this out."

"I'm good with that."

Frank switched off the TV and dropped the remote on his nightstand. "In the morning, we'll talk to the people at the morgue."

# CHAPTER ELEVEN

THE OXYGEN MASKS descended as alarms blared from every direction. Flashes of light spilled over the backs of seats from outside the airplane window. Faces tensed, eyes wide, mouths gaping.

Micah's limp body sunk into the chair like being strapped into a rollercoaster seat. Restrained, compressed with gravity, unable to move.

The woman with her emerald eyes and auburn hair screamed. She clung to Micah's arm.

Sinking.

Falling.

The force of gravity pulled his stomach down, pressing against his intestines. The sheer weight made him want to crap his pants. His eyes rolled back into his head, and pressure like a migraine thumped behind his eyes.

The airplane broke open into pieces, and the night air came rushing at him. As metal tore and splintered, sounds like the screeching of birds accompanied hunks of airplane disappearing into the darkness.

There, and then gone. Vaporized.

Pelting rain. Only his section of the plane remained, somehow afloat, carrying forward through the storm. Olivia had vanished, as had the hundreds of other passengers. Micah's seat then angled, plummeting toward the earth.

Alone, on a straight shot into the abyss.

His eyes opened.

He sat bolt upright in bed. A bead of sweat dribbled down the side of his face and clung to the underside of his chin. Chest constricted, difficulty breathing. The four walls around him were, at first, unfamiliar.

Motel. Not Denver. In Michigan. Across the room, Frank snorted and turned on his side, still asleep.

"Shit," Micah said as the three-hundred-pound jacket of anxiety lifted from him.

It had felt so real.

He wondered if Olivia was having the same dreams every night. If she also realized how close they'd come to crashing into the mountains, unable to stop it. Micah knew the statistics about how flying was safer than driving, and he also knew why people still feared airplanes. In a car, you have the illusion that you're in control, but while flying, it's completely out of your hands. You're at the mercy of the pilots and the weather and dumb luck.

He allowed his breathing to return to normal before rousting Frank out of bed so they could prepare to visit the morgue. They dressed in silence, both of them groggy, and then left to get coffee. Micah said he was fine with Starbucks, but Frank took him to some local spot named Good Beans.

They spoke little on the way, Micah still recovering from his dream and not wanting to speak about it. Frank wasn't dumb, though. He would glean from Micah's shaky appearance that he'd been rattled by something. But Frank didn't pester him, and Micah didn't offer any information.

Soon enough, they found themselves walking into the Genesee County Medical Examiner's office, pausing in a waiting room.

As Frank knocked on the steel door leading into the mortuary, Micah stood next to him and shuddered. Cold rolled through the cracks in the door, and his newly shaved head wasn't as insulating as having a full head of hair.

"You should let me do the talking," Frank said. "I know you're in disguise, but don't give these people any cause to look at you closely."

Micah's thoughts drifted to the ride over here. The streets of Flint were populated with almost nothing but American cars. He'd seen the occasional Volvo or Subaru, but mostly, Ford and Chevy, and usually late-model. When you live in a town built by cars, made sense to see that machinery flaunted everywhere.

Frank waved a hand in front of Micah's face. "You paying attention?"

"Sure, sure. I'm good. I'll keep my mouth shut."

"You should know," Frank said, "that his body is not in good shape. His face is untouched, but they cut him up bad below that. Burned him. Mutilated him. It's like sausage from the neck down."

Micah swallowed. Didn't know if he was ready to see that.

The door opened and there stood a squat man with slick black hair and glasses thicker than the fake ones Micah was wearing. Dressed in tie-dyed scrubs. The man eyed Frank and Micah, lingering a little longer at Micah. There was no way this guy would recognize him, though. Not with a shaved head, glasses, and fake blue eyes. At least, that's what Micah hoped.

"Good morning, gentlemen."

"I'm Frank Mueller from Mueller Bail Enforcement. This is my partner Roland Templeton," Frank said as he gestured at Micah.

"I'm Danny," the squat man in the scrubs said. "How can I help you?"

Frank flipped open his wallet to show his bounty hunter license, not that it would actually legitimize them being here. Maybe Danny wouldn't look at the license too closely.

"You're not the medical examiner."

Danny shook his head. "No sir. She's going to be late this morning."

"That's fine, I wanted to talk to you anyway. You met a woman a couple days ago. Anita Mueller, from the DOJ?"

"Mueller. Of course, I remember. She a relation to you?"

"Yes, she is. That's my sister. I was hoping I could ask you some follow-up questions regarding that John Doe you came across. The one she had you pull from your storage."

Danny hooked a thumb, pointing at rows of stainless steel vaults behind him. "Sure, but he's gone."

"He's what?" Micah said. "The body isn't here?"

"Yeah," Danny said, "he's gone. Your sister didn't give me any instructions to hold him, and we ran out of space."

Micah felt a rush of something he couldn't quite name. Relief, maybe, that he didn't have to look at this doppelgänger. And a bit of disappointment, because no matter how he knew it might bother him, he'd wanted to see the body. Wanted to stare into the eyes of someone who had his same face, for reasons he couldn't explain.

"That's fine," Frank said. "I'd still like to ask you a couple questions. May we come in?"

Danny shrugged and ushered them into a little room off to the side, with two chairs. Micah let Frank sit, and he stood behind his boss.

Frank let out a groan as his butt hit the chair. "Danny, I really only need to know one thing: has anyone else stopped by to see the body?"

Danny paused for a second, his breath whistling in his nose. "I don't know what's going on here, but I'm not a small-town idiot."

"No one claimed you were," Frank said.

"This is some kind of government thing. Like the John Doe was a CIA agent, or maybe FBI?"

Frank smiled, baring white teeth. "It's not that exciting."

"Hard for me to believe. I usually work night shift, so I'm used to things being all wacky when I come in at night sometimes, but I've never seen the visitor log messed with before. Not until your John Doe showed up. Is that what you're asking?"

Frank and Micah shared a look. A secret visitor. Someone from the cartel sent to verify the corpse's identity, most likely.

"That's good to know, Danny. Has anyone stopped by while you were on shift and asked to see the body?"

"Aside from your sister?"

"Yes, aside from my sister."

"Just that doctor."

A light went off inside Micah's head. Not only a visitor, but a doctor?

Then, an idea struck. "What kind?"

"That's the thing," Danny said. "He never actually said he was a doctor. But I've seen him before. I knew who he was. I'd met him once at this thing... this fundraising thing in Midtown last year."

"Plastic surgeon?" Micah said.

Danny narrowed his eyes, looking at Micah for the first time. "How did you know that?"

Micah shrugged. "Just a guess."

Frank took a pad of paper and a pencil from inside his jacket pocket and held it out to Danny. "Would you be able to write down his name for us? We need to ask him some follow-up questions. It's related to a bail case we're working."

Danny accepted the pad and pencil but hesitated. "I don't know about this. I haven't seen anything that proves you guys aren't spooks. As far as I know, I'm going to end up on a plane to Venezuela just for talking to you."

"Danny," Micah said, leaning closer. "That John Doe who came in… it's important that we find out who he was. We're not CIA or FBI or anything like that. Just a couple of interested parties who are trying to get justice for this dead man. You can help us with that."

Danny gripped the pencil, his eyes flicking back and forth between the two of them.

## CHAPTER TWELVE

ICAH AND FRANK stood outside the office of Dr. Herschel Spector, staring at the golden nameplate next to the glass door. Dr. Spector's office was a lone brick building, a one-story structure a few blocks from downtown Flint. Small parking lot out back, street access in the front.

Years of decay baked onto every surface.

"How do you want to play this?" Micah said.

"Our best advantage is that he doesn't know we're coming."

"But, he has to have assumed the cops or someone else would come talk to him. He's going to be guarded."

Frank wiped a line of sweat from the back of his neck. "You have a knack for this, kid. You still thinking about law enforcement?"

"Not even a little. I told you before that I thought about it when I was young, but I also wanted to be a race car driver and an astronaut. I've seen enough of the other side of law enforcement to have been poisoned off that, though."

"Fair enough," Frank said. "I think you should hang back, in the waiting room for a minute or two, and let me go in first. Even with your shaved head and glasses, he's bound to recognize you. He must have studied pictures of your face to cut up that kid to look like you."

"Makes sense."

"Let me put a little pressure on him first, then you come in and we'll back him into a corner."

"And how do we force him to give up the people who hired him?"

Frank shrugged. "I'm not sure yet. Odds are, he performed the surgery for some bad people. Maybe we offer him protection, maybe we threaten to turn him over to the cops. We'll have to play it by ear, see what he gives us. See what he's most afraid of, and then use it on him. Some people, you go for the stick right away. Some of them, you can dangle a little carrot first, see how big their eyes get."

A cold chill ran up Micah's back. As Michael McBriar, he'd used the same kinds of tactics when working inside the cartel, threatening rival dealers, forcing information out of them. Since becoming Micah Reed and living a new sober life, he never thought he'd need those tactics again. Manipulation, deceit, and then brute force when those didn't work.

"I can see that look on your face," Frank said. "Maybe it

feels underhanded, but that's the way it works. You can't just ask a bad guy to tell you what you want to know. He has to be convinced."

"I know it, I just don't like it." Micah pushed his new fake glasses up the bridge of his nose into position. "I'm ready, though."

Frank opened the door to a small waiting area, about the size of a living room. Collection of couches lining the walls, and a cutaway with a desk on one side. A gray-haired lady sat behind the desk, chains dangling from the rims of her glasses.

"Can I help you, gentlemen?" she said as Micah retreated to a seat on one of the couches. No sense in letting the receptionist recognize him right off the bat and ruining their upper hand.

"Yes," Frank said. "Is Dr. Spector in today?"

"Do you have an appointment?"

"No ma'am. Is he busy?"

She held up a finger and picked up the phone, then mumbled something into the receiver. She nodded, then hung up. "Okay, you can go on in." She pointed to the only other door, an opaque glass one in the corner.

Frank gave Micah a look and mouthed, "two minutes," before thanking the receptionist and disappearing into the doctor's office.

Micah avoided eye contact with the receptionist as he thumbed through magazines on a coffee table in front of him. Mostly about golf, one of those sports Micah didn't consider a sport. If you could drink beer and smoke cigarettes while playing, you couldn't convince him it was an actual sport.

He checked the time on a wall clock, and sixty seconds had passed since Frank had walked through that door. No voices came through the walls. Sixty seconds of silence and the unknown.

What if the doctor had jammed a syringe into Frank's neck? Frank could be dying on this man's office floor, right at this moment.

Five more seconds passed.

Five more.

Micah closed his eyes, pulling deep breaths in through his nose and letting them eke out his mouth. Rapid pulse thumped inside his neck, but he didn't know why. He had no reason to think Frank couldn't handle himself.

"Looks like rain out there today, eh?" the receptionist said.

Something in the doctor's office crashed. Muffled sounds of an argument came through the walls.

Micah shot to his feet and leaped over the coffee table, knocking the golf magazines to the floor. He dashed across the room. His shoulder slammed into the door, and he barely managed to close his hand around the knob.

After he'd flung open the door, Micah stumbled in to see Frank bent back over the desk, his shoulders pinned. A man in a white lab coat stood over Frank, meaty hands wrapped around his throat. The attacker was furious, babbling, his eyes bulging out of their sockets. Spittle flew from his lips onto Frank's face.

Frank was swinging an arm against the doctor's burly frame, but his punches seemed to have no effect. Each blow sunk into a mountain of clothed flesh.

The doctor hadn't seemed to have noticed Micah's entrance.

Micah spun around and his eyes landed on a table near the door, topped with a collection of items. A plastic skull, cut away in sections to reveal a brain inside. A football with faded autographs etched below the laces. And an object that was made of glass, about eight inches tall, in the shape of a slender pyramid.

Micah snatched the glass pyramid. His eyes landed on the words *To Dr. Herschel Spector* engraved at the bottom. Instead of pausing to read the rest, Micah swung it at the doctor in one motion, cracking the base of it into Spector's head.

Now the doctor noticed him.

He released his grip on Frank's throat as his hands flew to the spot Micah had smacked him. Blood filled a tiny hole above his eyebrow. The doctor stumbled back a couple steps, wailing from the pain.

He turned around, and when his eyes met Micah's, he went as white as a glass of milk. Mouth fell open, revealing a collection of gold crowns.

"You," Dr. Spector said. Balled his fists. His eyes darted around, and then he threw his hands at Micah's chest, leveraging his full weight behind the blow.

Caught off guard, Micah had no time to deflect the attack. He fell backward, his tailbone connecting with the table. The football tumbled to the ground. Burst of pain shot up his spine.

Micah saw stars from the pain for at least a full second. By the time he'd recovered, the doctor was rushing out of the office, brushing past Micah.

Micah tried to grasp the man as he fled, but the pain in his back had dulled his reaction time. It took another endless second for him to gather his wits. Through the closed door, he could hear the doctor barking at his receptionist.

Frank was still on the table, his hands around his own throat. Micah rushed to his side, and Frank pushed himself upright. His face was flushed, his chest heaving.

"I'm fine," came Frank's throaty and deep voice. "Go after him, kid. You let that doctor leave, we'll never see him again."

Micah left Frank there alone and raced out of the office, into the reception room, as the building's front door slammed. The little old lady at the desk was shouting, but Micah couldn't make out a word of it. He did hear Frank behind him, lumbering to rise to his feet.

Micah barreled forward, but he hit a roadblock when the door wouldn't open. The doctor had locked it behind him.

Precious seconds were disappearing. Micah fumbled with the door until he found the deadbolt to unlock it. He flung it open and ran out of the office, into the street. Barely managed to avoid not being flattened by a passing

Corvette. The honk of its horn momentarily jarred his brain.

Looked left and right. No sign of the doctor.

Micah picked a direction and ran, cutting around the side of the building and doubling back. The parking lot was behind the office, and he had to assume the doctor would go for his car.

Micah needed to get there first.

"I'm right behind you," Frank shouted as Micah made the last turn into the parking lot.

Micah glanced around the lot, and realization smacked him like a frying pan. Doctor Spector was there. Sitting, leaning up against a brand-new Chevy Malibu, his throat cut. Blood spilling down over his lab coat.

One minute ago, this man had been alive. Someone else had been waiting for him.

Frank came to a stop next to Micah.

"He knew right away," Frank said. "Knew exactly why I was there. Big son of a bitch jumped me."

Micah spun around in the parking lot, looking for anything that might explain what had happened. Suicide was possible, but there was no bloody knife nearby, no other sign of a weapon.

Out of the corner of his eye, he caught a flash of color. Two men racing toward a truck, growling at each other to hurry up. They hadn't seen Micah and Frank, they were too busy scurrying through the parking lot. One of the men tossed a backpack into the bed of the truck, and then they both jumped into the cab. Micah scrambled to free his phone from his pocket.

As the truck peeled out of the parking lot, he managed to raise the phone and snap a picture before it joined the street and disappeared.

He checked his phone. Spread two fingers to zoom into the picture, and he could see the faces of the two men. "I got it, Frank. I got a picture of them."

"Let me see that."

Micah handed the phone over and fished the rental car keys out of his pocket. "Do we go after them?"

"Son of a bitch."

"What?" Micah said.

"No need to go after them. I know exactly where we can find these two."

# CHAPTER THIRTEEN

OLIVIA STOOD OUTSIDE of the back door of the Chinese restaurant, wiping perspiration from her brow. A collection of dampness had pooled just above her tailbone. "Isn't it a little early for it to be this hot?"

Jeremy fumbled in his back pocket to retrieve his handkerchief for her. "It's the humidity from the lakes. Michigan is always cold and wet or hot and wet. Plus, we came from Denver, which is one of the driest places in the country."

"Weatherman Jeremy to the rescue."

He shrugged and gave her the handkerchief, which she used to wipe the sweat and blood off her hands. The fact that some of the blood would stick under her fingernails grossed her out. Wasn't the first time, though.

"You ready to go back in," she asked, "or want to let him stew a minute more?"

"He can stew. Gives me a chance to clear something up." He paused to take a contemplative breath. "What were you hoping to get out of talking to that club owner Tyson Darby, back in Denver? You never told me."

"I thought I'd heard that he and Micah Reed were mixed up together. I was sure of it."

"Why does it matter one way or another if he was working for this Tyson character?"

"Because," Olivia said, "I like to have all the pieces together. But you're right. It doesn't matter. Doesn't change what we do when we catch up to Micah."

"I thought you were maybe just trying to stir the pot with Darby."

She smirked. "Well, there was that, too. I did have fun, sitting at that table, pointing my gun at his crotch."

Jeremy nodded, then he did that thing where he swished his lips back and forth, like he had a mouth full of Listerine. Usually meant he was debating how to phrase whatever it was he wanted.

"Something on your mind?"

"Yes. Last night."

Olivia rubbed her eyes and sighed. "What happened last night happened. I don't want to keep making a big deal out of it. Which means if you can't keep things in perspective, then we're going to have to stop doing that."

He gritted his teeth. "I don't see how you can come into my hotel room in the middle of the night, slide into my bed, and then leave right after. Then you won't say a word about it, and we go back to business-as-usual every morning. How am I supposed to keep that in perspective?"

She was, at least, grateful he wasn't trying to use the *treating-me-like-a-piece-of-meat* argument.

"Because it *is* business as usual," she said. "I don't get why you have to keep bringing it up as if somehow my position on this is going to change."

He opened his mouth to respond, but only air leaked out. After a few seconds of this, his face turned cold. Olivia sighed, because even though she knew her late night hotel room visits kept complicating things, she wished he could *man up* and start seeing it for what it was. A fling. An occasional tension-reliever. Weren't men supposed to love that no-strings freebie stuff?

He nodded and tilted his head at the door. "That's all I wanted to say. I'm ready to go back in for round two."

His terse response meant the conversation would be continued at some future date, and that was fine. As long as they didn't have to hash it out right now.

They entered the restaurant through the kitchen, amid the jungle of pots and pans and canned goods stacked up to the ceiling. But most importantly, Mr. Kim was still tied to the fryer, sweat dripping down his round face. The fryer was nestled against the wall between a pair of stainless steel cutting tables, with Kim's hand bound to the side.

He'd slunk down into a crouch, his arm craned above his head at an awkward angle because of the zip tie. Chest quaking, bruises on his face already turning purple.

"Mr. Kim," Olivia said. "Have you reconsidered?"

"Go to hell," he said. "I don't have to say anything. My wife will be here in half hour, so if you are going to kill me, please do quickly, then take my body out back. She already have heart attack last year and don't need to see me dead."

"We're not going to kill you," Olivia said.

Kim bared his teeth. "Then let me go, you assholes."

Olivia motioned to Jeremy and he dipped a spoon into the fryer full of bubbling golden brown liquid. He only brought out a half teaspoon of the liquid, but it would be enough. He flicked the drops at Mr. Kim. The boiling lard splashed against his cheek, and he wailed as it trickled down and dirtied his white chef's coat.

"Monster," Mr. Kim blubbered. "You people are monsters."

Olivia crossed her arms. "You're doing this to yourself. All I want to know is if you and your people were in Bassett Park on the 15th. That's it. We know your little gang slings meth and coke in that area."

"If you want territory," Mr. Kim said, "you can have it. It's a shitty neighborhood anyway. Poor business."

Olivia nodded, and Jeremy spooned more drops of fryer lard onto Mr. Kim's head. He groaned and tried to squirm away, but he did not beg for mercy. Why was this little Asian man so damn stubborn?

"You're still not listening to me," she said. "I don't care about your small-fry powder operation and I don't want your customers. I'm onto bigger fish. I want to know if you were in the park that night. A body turned up there, all shot up, burned, cut into pieces. A body that got dumped at the Genesee County Medical Examiner's office as a John Doe. You know the one I'm talking about?"

Mr. Kim twisted up his sweaty face in surprise.

She dropped to a knee, looking deep into Kim's haggard eyes. He had no idea what she was talking about. No way could he have faked that face after what they'd done to him.

"I don't know," he said. "We didn't kill no one in the park."

So if this fake Micah Reed wasn't killed by Mr. Kim and his little drug operation, then who killed him? Had Micah done it himself to try to collect the bounty on his own head?

"That would be ballsy," she muttered. "And unlikely."

"What?" Jeremy said.

Olivia shook her head. "We're done here." She motioned for Jeremy to cut Kim's zip tie. Jeremy dragged a knife across the plastic ties, and Mr. Kim collapsed to the ground as soon as his bonds were cut. Didn't try to get up. Instead, he groaned and wept softly to himself on the floor.

Olivia tilted her head toward the back door, and Jeremy followed her out of the restaurant.

"What was that all about?" he said. "Why did you stop?"

"I had a feeling this might be a waste of time, but now we know for sure. It wasn't him or his people. I'm thinking either Micah Reed did in this lookalike himself, or our original theory was correct."

"Which way are you leaning?" Jeremy said.

"I don't know, but it makes sense to tail Micah until we

know for sure, so we're going to stay on him. Make sure he doesn't mess things up."

"But we know where he's staying. If you're concerned about his involvement, shouldn't we go ahead and pick him up?"

She considered it. Wanted to keep her options open. "I'd rather not make ourselves known to him if we don't have to. Not yet, at least."

CHAPTER FOURTEEN

ROURKE PATTERSON LIFTED the steak and onion sub to his face and dug in, red sauce dripping from the corners of his mouth onto the table. He and his two friends Carter and Ethan liked to eat at the Big John Steak and Onion on Dort Highway, not only for the sub sandwiches, but also because it put them across the street from the Dort Mall, their target.

Well, not the mall itself, but underneath the mall.

For a long time now, they'd been coming here, investigating, learning what they could. Weeks had bled into months. Rourke could feel it in his bones that now was the time to strike. All of the hesitation and second-guessing had led them in circles. They had a million excuses to keep delaying.

Besides the three of them, only one other person was eating at the Big John that afternoon. They kept the conversation limited to the Detroit Lions' draft choices until that man left, and then Rourke got down to business.

"We need to settle on a date," Rourke said. "I feel like once we have a date, it'll be easier to get everything together. And I don't mean a date six weeks from now. I mean a date like this weekend."

Carter pushed his glasses up his nose and ran a hand through his long blonde hair. "This weekend? Having a date won't help if we can't acquire the guns in time."

"We have guns," Ethan said.

"We need more," Carter said. "Automatic weapons, not pea-shooters. I want this just as much as you two, but not unless we do it right."

Rourke wiped the grease from his hands on a napkin and took a long pull from his Dr. Pepper. Carter had a point, but Rourke wasn't going to be swayed this time. "We'll find a way to get what we need."

Carter ignored this and squinted at Rourke's sub. "Did you not get the pickles?"

"I did *not* get the pickles on it," Rourke said.

"Why not?"

Rourke shrugged.

"Dude, you have to get the pickles. Not getting the pickles is like getting a hand job when you could be slipping your meat into the glorious cave. Sure, a handy will get the job done, but think of what you're missing."

Ethan cleared his throat. "Totally. You have to get the pickles. I knew this great sub place above the bridge, in

Marquette. Good pirogies, too, if you can deal with all that. Lake people, know what I mean?"

"I don't want to talk about the pickles anymore," Rourke said. "If we have a date to go in the casino, then we'll *have* to get the guns. Having a deadline makes everything real, and that's what we've been missing. All this dicking around, the what-ifs and problems."

"Look," Carter said, "I know this is your deal. I know how important this is to you. And it's important to me that we do it right, because the consequences are serious. I don't want you to think me and Ethan are only in it for the money—"

"Because we're not," Ethan said.

Carter sighed. "I know it's about more than that."

Rourke knew exactly what it was about for him. His two friends had stuck by him these last few months of planning, and their interest had never come up. "What does it mean to you?"

"Getting paid, obviously," Carter said. "Getting these interlopers out of our neighborhood. Making this a safe place to live again."

Rourke had no idea what *interlopers* meant, but he liked the way Carter had said it.

Ethan tore into his Spicy Italian sub and swallowed a giant lump. "They deserve every bad thing that happens to them. I'm all for helping that process along."

"But having a deadline doesn't mean anything if it's an arbitrary date that we don't use," Carter said.

Rourke grinned. "*Arbitrary.* You always did like your fifty cent words."

"We get the guns, and *then* we decide on a date," Carter said.

Rourke set down his soda too quickly, splashing some brown liquid on his tray. "No. I've made up my mind, so this is how it's going to be. We go in three days. We're just going to have to make it work, and all the other bullshit can take a backseat."

Carter sat back and crossed his arms, shaking his head. "Ethan, are you okay with that?"

"Sure," Ethan said as he checked the date on his phone. "I mean... how tough can it be, really? We bust in, take out the muscle, and then we snatch the kitty. Maybe we have to pull a trigger, or maybe we can get the drop on them and it's not even necessary. If we're going in on Saturday night, there should be a shit-ton of money to be had. Seems like a good plan to me."

Rourke pointed at Ethan while he eyed Carter. "Ethan here gets it. Time is short, my friend. We're going to hit these bastards hard, and they'll never see it coming."

The lone employee at the Big John poked his head out from behind the counter as he refilled a bin with ketchup packets. Rourke and his friends hushed their conversations. The employee looked at them with a cocked eye, but he didn't say anything about it. In another moment, he retreated back behind the counter, and the three conspirators leaned closer over the table and hushed their voices.

"Never see it coming?" Carter said. "First of all, we have

to find a way to access the basement floor, which is guarded. And then we have to actually get into the casino, which is also going to be guarded. We start popping off shots, and all the easy ways in and out close up. We'll have to shoot our way out like a James Bond movie. You're a handsome man, Rourke, but you're no James Bond."

Rourke smacked Carter in the arm. "You think too much. We know they cash out around two in the morning. And we know once they take the kitty out, it's in an armored truck, in a convoy. Right?"

"Right," Carter said. "Once it's on that truck, it's gone to who knows where."

"So we have to hit them about a quarter to two. Most of the gamblers have packed up and gone home, maybe even some of the muscle has left."

"And are we supposed to sneak in the mall like we're there to play the slots?" Carter said. He hooked a thumb at Ethan. "I don't know if you could tell by his curly black hair or his last name ending with *berg*, but Ethan is not exactly their type. The guys who run this place aren't equal opportunity businessmen, if you know what I'm saying."

Ethan wrapped up his half-eaten sub and shoved it in the front pocket of his hoodie. "Nazi shitbags."

"I'm thinking of a way around that," Rourke said. "Maybe we don't try the frontal assault method."

"Have you been inside lately?" Ethan said. "Like, do you know how many we're going to be dealing with?"

Rourke sat back and thought about how he wanted to answer that question. He didn't want to tell them about going to the casino in the basement of the Dort Mall with his dad. Didn't want to tell them about watching his dad waste his college fund at the poker table while Rourke played with his Matchbox cars in the corner of the enormous and smoky room. Blinking lights and twinkling sounds from all directions. Didn't want to tell them about seeing his dad being dragged off into a back room, then emerging hours later, his face a bruised and bloodied mess. Shaking him awake. *Wake up, Rourkey. It's time to go home and go to sleep in your own bed.*

"I've been inside," Rourke said, and left it at that.

# CHAPTER FIFTEEN

MICAH AND FRANK sat in the rental car, engine idling. Micah's newly shaved head itched, and the glasses weighed heavily on his nose.

They surveyed the husk of the Dort Mall, a place as barren as an old drive-in movie theater. Maybe a half dozen cars in the parking lot clustered together like Koi in a pond. Weeds had sprung up through cracks in the concrete. Scattered trash occupied many of the parking spaces.

Reminded Micah of one of those *last services for next eighty miles* gas stations you'd see on highways, dropped in the middle of nowhere. A business begging for people to pay attention to it, but its pleas were falling on deaf ears.

Frank pointed at the car keys and Micah killed the engine.

"What a dump," Micah said.

"It's hard to argue that it's not, looking like such a pile of crap. Wasn't always like this, though. Dort used to be quite a happening kind of place. Stores, restaurants, kids being delinquents in the parking lots, just like a regular mall."

"The casino room is literally underground?"

Frank nodded. "Let me see your phone again."

Micah handed over the phone and Frank opened the picture Micah had snapped of the two men getting into the truck, right after they had sliced open the throat of the plastic surgeon. Or, he assumed they'd done it. No way to know for sure without asking them.

"Haven't seen this bastard in at least twenty-five years," Frank said as he tapped on the face of one of the men, "but I recognize him as clear as day. I was drinking back then, but I know it's him. Hair's a little thinner up top, face is a little fuller, but no mistaking it. I don't remember his name, but he works for a guy that calls himself Harvey. Harvey's the owner and proprietor of this establishment."

"Harvey," Micah said, musing on the name. Seemed harmless.

"But our guy here was a bruiser for this gang that calls themselves Crossroads. Harvey is also the boss of the gang. Skinheads, but they're the new kind of skinheads that don't actually have shaved heads. Gambling, mostly, but back then they were into drugs and a bit of prostitution."

"Mafia sampler platter," Micah said.

Frank chuckled. "Yep."

"And this casino under the mall is where they operate from?"

"Used to be, back in the day. I assume it's still there, but that's what we're here to find out. I'm guessing we're going to discover our guy and Harvey down there."

Micah drummed his hands on the steering wheel, then ran his index finger over the bump that Boba Fett's head made in his jeans pocket. "So these people—these Crossroads people—paid a plastic surgeon to cut up some poor guy to look like me, probably so they could collect a bounty on my head from the cartel."

Frank erupted with a barrage of coughs so intense that tears streamed down his face by the time he was through. "Looks that way."

"You okay?" Micah said.

"Fine, kid."

Micah sighed at the dirty windows of the mall. "I don't like this."

"I don't like it much, either. But getting access to whatever is going on with these people is the next logical step. We don't have any warm leads to follow."

"I get it. I'm ready to go in if you are."

Frank shook his head. "It's best if you stay out of it. Why don't you poke around outside, and I'll go in and find out what I can. Even if they don't recognize you as being you, with your fake contacts and your nerd glasses, they probably saw you snap their picture back there at the doctor's office."

"They didn't see me. I was watching them the whole time."

"Even so, better safe than sorry. I'll still go in by myself. This may turn out to be nothing, and better to keep you removed from that. If we keep you out of sight, that lets us hold on to our element of surprise."

"But, Frank, you said they're skinheads. Like, neo-nazis."

Frank nodded. "I did say that."

"No offense, but you're kinda the wrong color to walk into a skinhead casino."

Frank laughed. "I'm aware of that. Don't you worry about me. My skin may be black, but my money is green, so I think I'll be okay. And if not, I picked this up at a pawn shop before you got here." Frank popped the glove box and took out a .357 Magnum revolver.

Micah paused to ask himself if he was upset about not going in because he was genuinely concerned about Frank, or because he didn't want to be out of the loop. The answer came back: yes, he was worried about Frank. Seemed like the old man was about to dive into a nest of vipers.

"Please try not to shoot up the place. You might need more than six bullets to get out safely."

"I hear what you're saying," Frank said. "I'm just going to slip in there and see if anything raises any red flags. I'll keep a low profile, I promise."

"The murder of this plastic surgeon might not have anything to do with us. Could be a coincidence. We could be connecting threads that have nothing to do with each other."

"Maybe. Then again, might *not* be a coincidence."

Micah watched his mentor spin the revolver's cylinder. A pain tickled the back of his neck. He had a feeling Frank wasn't going to get in and out so easily.

"If you're not out in a half hour," Micah said, "I'm going in after you. I don't care if they recognize me or not."

"Fair enough, kid. Let's do this."

# CHAPTER SIXTEEN

FRANK STEPPED OVER the threshold into the Dort Mall. Dust infiltrated his nostrils. He sneezed, sending the sound echoing along the corridors. The mall was a barren place, stuck in time, with most of the shops closed. When Frank had lived here and frequented this mall—over a quarter century ago—Dort had been a lively spot full of people and commerce. Now it was a carcass of what it used to be.

The only way you could tell it was the same place was the insane decor running the length of the interior of the mall. The owner had spent a lifetime collecting antiques and oddities and had displayed them here, plastered on the walls, hanging from the ceiling, in the hallways.

Glowing neon signs. Sports equipment. The wings and propellers of prop planes hanging above as if they were in mid-flight. Road signs collected from a cross-section of American highways. A merry go round in the center of a large room. A giant wooden elephant and a twenty-foot Tyrannosaurus rex made of car parts. It was like the inside of a deranged mad scientist/antique store owner's head, with bits and pieces of miscellaneous Americana shot from a nostalgia cannon everywhere.

Frank had to strain his memories to the tearing point to remember where the damn entrance to the casino was. Basement somewhere. It had been a dance club at one point, then closed up and made to look sealed off when it had become the casino.

Last time he'd been here, though, there were shoppers everywhere, stores pumping music. This was like a ghost town. The main area of the mall was one long room, a massive rectangle with store windows lining each side. Some skinny hallways branched off, but most of it was in plain view.

He walked along the main area of the mall, the heels of his shoes clacking on the painted cement like cracks of a whip, echoing in all directions. He could hear the wheeze of air in and out of his nostrils.

Up ahead was the sporting goods store. Hockey place. He remembered this establishment, and it seemed to be one of the only things still in business. If the entrance was in the same place, he seemed to recall that he could access the casino through an entrance past the hockey shop, near the mall janitorial closet.

Maybe there was an outside entrance too, but he couldn't be sure. Was there some way to gain entry through the hockey store itself? That sounded familiar.

He passed the hockey shop and eyed the janitor's closet where the mall floor dead-ended. Caught curious looks from employees inside the store as he walked on by. They probably hadn't seen anyone come to this end of the mall but not go into their shop in years.

He tried the door handle to the closet and found it locked. Bit his lower lip. Micah was good at picking locks, but Frank didn't want to risk bringing the kid in here. Not until he knew for sure if this Crossroads gang was involved in killing that Micah lookalike or not.

Frank wandered back to the store, and the employees who'd been near the front had left. He poked his head in and noticed there were six of them, huddled off to the side, almost out of sight. Team meeting, or something like that.

His memory sputtered and kicked, not wanting to give in and recover the alternate entrance. He couldn't figure it out. Instead, he used some old cop logic and relied on a hunch. It would make sense for an entrance to lead from somewhere in this hockey store. Manager's office, most likely.

Frank took a chance and hurried across the room, toward the back. A piercing ache squeezed his stomach. He'd been hurting like this almost constantly, all morning. Maybe he shouldn't have had that second breakfast burrito, even as meager as the damn things had looked.

He reached the back of the store without attracting any attention and opened the manager's office. Giant room inside with desks and a twenty-person conference table. Bits of unused mall decor sat about in this room too: one of those Depression-era boardwalk *love tester* machines, some old-timey bicycles with the comically oversized front wheels, and a collection of lamps with bases shaped like legs.

Where the hell had all this crap come from? Who spends so much time and money to turn a place into some elderly person's garage?

And, at the far end of the room, a door marked *basement*. Now he remembered that door, like suddenly coming up with the name of an actor on television that's been eluding you for hours.

The rest of the memories materialized. Frank recalled coming here more than once as a cop for noise complaints, getting the guided tour, only to find nothing illegal or out of place. Smiling faces. *Nothing untoward going on here, officer.*

He opened the door and descended a set of stairs lit only by a single overhead light. No handrail to guide him. The stairs felt slick, and he traced a hand down the wall to keep his balance. He could see a turn at the bottom and light coming from the left, and when he reached it, a man at a desk at the end of a hallway perked up.

The man jumped to his feet and slid a hand into his suit pocket. "Can I help you, sir?"

Frank took a few steps toward him, but carefully, so he wouldn't spook the guy. Seemed like the jumpy type. "Just so we're clear about what I'm doing, I'm going to reach in my back pocket for my wallet."

"Slowly, please."

Frank removed his wallet and drew five twenties. He fanned them out and took a few more steps toward the guard.

The guard stiffened, but let his eyes fall to the bills. Like a cat to catnip. He didn't want to look, but Frank could practically smell the saliva welling at the back of the gatekeeper's throat.

"Do you know where you are, sir?"

Frank nodded.

"And if you know that, I would have to assume you know who runs this place."

Frank nodded again, even though he wasn't sure, and that's what he was here to find out. Still, he kept his face even and confident.

"Then you must know we don't typically let in people of your… type."

"That's fine, and I understand people of my type don't usually find themselves in this hallway. I'm just here to have some fun. I don't want any trouble. I can spend my money elsewhere if that's going to be a problem."

Frank held out the bills. "This is a gift for you, by the way."

The man hesitated, then tilted his head at the desk. Frank dropped the bills.

"When you go inside, you'll need a password. The password today is *sallow*."

"Swallow?"

"No, sallow."

"*Sallow?*"

"That's right."

The man waved Frank on to a door behind him, never taking his hand out of his coat pocket. Frank did his best not to startle him because the guy seemed one car backfire away from launching out of his skin.

Frank eased through the door and into something like a living room, with a couple chairs and a sofa, straight out of the seventies. Lime green and fuzzy. He didn't remember this waiting room from before but it had been an eternity since he'd been here.

Another white man, just like the one outside this room, stood in front of another desk. But this man wore his gun on the outside. Submachine gun on a strap across his chest. And instead of nervous, this one was as still as a statue. Big square jaw and broad chest.

Frank knew his type by his expression. This one couldn't be bought.

The man's fingers flew to the grip of the gun, but he didn't raise it. His eyes stayed dim and focused.

"Password. Now," The man said, his finger hovering above the trigger.

"Sallow."

The man took his fingers off the grip and let them fall to his sides. Adopted a grin as his eyes opened enough for Frank to notice they were blue. Now they seemed like old buddies.

He pointed at a door behind him. "Right this way, sir. Welcome to our little club."

"Thanks. This club have a name?"

"It does not, sir."

Frank walked to the door, but the man raised his arm, blocking him. "I'll need to search you, sir."

"I'm an old man," Frank said, trying to look pathetic. "What damage do you think I'm gonna do in there, son?"

"I still need to search you."

"Okay, then," Frank said as he lifted up his arms. No way would this guy miss Frank's gun with even a cursory search. Time to think of a distraction, and be quick about it.

The man placed his hands under Frank's armpits and slid them down. Frank had no idea how to stop him. He couldn't overpower the big guy.

As the meaty bruiser started to reach around the back of Frank's waist, Frank threw his elbow into the man's nose, a half second before he would have discovered the revolver in the back of Frank's waistband.

The man's hands rushed to his face and he stumbled back. Frank yanked the pistol from his belt and flipped it to grab it by the barrel, then he smashed the grip against the man's face. Nose bones crunched and blood pooled above his upper lip.

The man opened his mouth to cry out, so Frank jabbed him in the chin. Felt his own knuckle crack. The man crumbled, then slipped, and fell on the desk, his head smacking against it. He slumped to the floor, out cold.

Frank put a couple fingers against the guy's neck to check for a pulse. Found one. Figured he might have three minutes, maybe four, until this man woke up again.

"Shit."

This wasn't how this was supposed to go. He'd wanted to look around and get a feel for the place, but now he'd started something irreversible. No time to worry about that now, though. He had to make some use out of this trip before getting the hell out of here.

He opened the door into the casino.

Dim overhead lights. No windows. Poker tables, roulette, blinking and clinking slot machines. Not too crowded, maybe thirty or forty people gambling. A thin haze of cigarette smoke in the air. Frank was definitely the only non-white person here. A half dozen girls in skimpy outfits carrying trays of drinks from table to table. And at least ten men in sharp suits, standing at strategic angles to those tables, coiled wires sticking from their ears.

And across the room, chatting with one of those girls in the skimpy outfits, stood Harvey and the man from Micah's picture, the one fleeing the scene of the plastic surgeon's murder.

# CHAPTER SEVENTEEN

MICAH CIRCLED THE Dort Mall on foot, keeping his eyes on the pale purple awning that ran the length of the exterior. The wind picked up every few seconds, ruffling the awning like the hem of a dress. It was a sort of faded color that suggested a lack of upkeep and years of relentless bleaching from the sun.

Denver was such a shining beacon of capitalism and wealth that seeing the city of Flint in this state of decay didn't compute for Micah. He wasn't used to barren parking lots and empty, dilapidated buildings. A lack of enthusiasm for upkeep.

Denver had a homeless population, but those people usually had somewhere to go to escape the cold nights. Did they have the same here? Or was the city too broken to care for its least-valuable citizens? Some places, they swept them under the rug like dust bunnies.

As he rounded a corner to the back of the mall, he found himself looking at a long parking lot with a couple big rigs parked, one of them backed up to a loading dock on the far side. The other big rig was not attached to a bay, rather, it sat as an island on its own. Probably some trucker sleeping off a bad drunk in the cab.

Opposite the parking lot was a wall of those massive and pointy trees. The trees kept the Dort Mall hemmed in, when otherwise, it might try to flee to a more prosperous location.

Out of the corner of his eye, Micah caught the only element with any life or motion to it. A group of three guys huddled together near the outside of the mall. One of them was pressing a notebook up against the building, scribbling, while the other two pointed at it. They were collaborating, or arguing, or both.

One was roughly Micah's same height and build, one was scrawny with long blond hair, and the other a tall and thick guy with curly black hair. All of them seemed mid-twenties. Maybe late twenties.

As Micah studied their features, he lost track of where he was walking and accidentally kicked a stray beer bottle. It skidded away from his foot and the noise echoed off the building.

The average-looking kid stopped what he was doing and cradled the notebook against his chest. Protected it like a secret. They all glared at Micah as they converged into a line, as if expecting an attack. Either that, or a game of Red Rover. Kind of a sloppy group to be standing out in the open, conducting their business for anyone to see.

"What do you want?" said the tall kid with curly hair. He balled his fists, trying to look intimidating. He did a decent job of it, actually.

The average-looking one held out a hand across the tall one's stomach. "It's cool, Ethan." Then, to Micah: "Are you lost, man? There's nothing to see back here. Mall entrance is on the front side."

"I know where it is. I'm just looking."

"Not going to find anything back here but used condoms and broken bottles," said the scrawny one.

"How do you know that's not what I'm looking for?"

The average one smiled. "Fair enough. What's your name?"

"Micah."

"Okay, Micah, I'm Rourke. So which is it? Condoms or bottles?"

The scrawny one scowled as he swept the blond hair out of his eyes. "What are you doing? This guy doesn't need to know your name."

Micah held up the palms of his hands, a show of surrender. He could tell by how wound-up all of them were that they were up to something. They clearly hadn't expected anyone to interrupt the grand plan they were orchestrating. "Whatever you guys are into, I couldn't care less. I'm not here to cause any trouble. You may want to consider a more secluded spot, though, if it's something you don't want everyone to see."

Big guy didn't like that. "You need to mind your own damn business."

"Like I mentioned," Micah said, shrugging, "I'm just looking. I'm not trying to be up in your business."

The blond one crossed his arms and stared in a way that made Micah a little uncomfortable. "Do I know you?"

"I doubt it," Micah said. "I'm not from around here."

"If you're not here for us," Rourke said, "then what *are* you looking for?"

Micah said nothing, since he didn't quite know himself.

"Maybe you should keep on walking," said Ethan, the big guy. "Get your bottles and condoms and leave us be."

Even though he'd said he didn't care, Micah did now feel the hint of an itch to ask. Hard not to. With how defensive they'd all been, it had to be something illegal. Still, their plans weren't Micah's business, and he didn't have any right to ask.

Ethan took a step forward because apparently Micah wasn't responding to his command quickly enough.

"Okay, guys, have a good one," Micah said. He dug his hands into his pockets and pivoted on his heels. In a few seconds, he was out of their earshot, and glanced back to see them once again hovering over the notebook. Planning something.

Micah strolled along the back of the mall, looking for clues or anything useful he could glean. It was a typical parking lot. Scattered ponds of broken windshield glass, discarded fast food bags, bits of paper blowing in the spring breeze. The occasional piece of tire rubber, but otherwise, nothing useful.

A hundred feet down the backside of the mall, away from the defensive kids, Micah strolled by a door with no markings. It came flying open, and there stood Frank, at the top of a staircase. Panicked expression, the fingers of his hands tensed like claws.

"Micah," he said, panting. "We got to go. We're not welcome here."

# CHAPTER EIGHTEEN

LIGHTS FLASHING, ALARMS blaring. Passengers screaming.

The front of the plane bowed and then snapped open. Like a twig with too much weight on one end, it bent under invisible pressure and then tore as the front half dipped into blackness.

Ahead of Micah was open air, sheets of rain slicing the night sky. Cold and black. With no cabin to hold their seats in place, passengers tumbled out of the severed front of the plane. Their faces spiraled into the darkness below, their wails fading as they spun out of view.

Micah's brain shouted at him to flee from his seat and sprint to the back of the plane, that he would be safe there. Ahead, seats dropped into nothingness as the fractured airplane folded back on itself like a candy bar unwrapping. The plane grew shorter and shorter, the darkness approaching Micah's position. Hunks of metal screamed through the air like rockets. Wind whipped his hair back. Then Micah realized he shouldn't have any hair. Hadn't he shaved his head when he'd come to Michigan?

He had to get out. Get to the back of the plane. Get to safety.

The number of screams around him diminished as more and more of his fellow passengers evaporated. The remaining people started to blur, their faces turning into fleshy messes.

Had to get out. But he couldn't unbuckle his seatbelt. He pressed the button but it wouldn't budge. With the pelting rain drenching his body, his hands slipped as they stabbed at the button. He felt heavy and unable to move. Helpless. The seconds slowed, and from somewhere, a clock counted time.

*Tick. Tick. Tick.*

He saw his death coming, and could do nothing to stop it. The row in front of him tore away and fell into the abyss.

Then he snapped awake.

Teeth gritted in anguish, hands gripping chunks of his dampened bedsheet. Sweat trickled from his temple to his chin. He could breathe, and he was inside, not flying through space.

The room materialized around him like a television fading in. Beds. Nightstands. Dressers. A framed art print of a ship coming into port hung on the beige wall.

Motel. Michigan.

A thin slice of light came in through a gap in the motel room curtain. Micah squinted over at Frank's bed, but he didn't detect a shape underneath the floral comforter. He waited a second for his bleary eyes to adjust, but he still didn't see Frank. No movement at all on that side of the room.

Micah snatched his phone from the nightstand and checked the time. Early morning. They'd retired last night after an AA meeting, and Frank hadn't mentioned anything about going out this morning. He wouldn't have left without letting Micah know beforehand.

Micah scrolled through his phone's notifications and saw no texts or emails from Frank. Nothing since the voicemail from three days ago, when Frank had thought he was staring at Micah's dead body on a slab in the morgue.

His eyes flicked over to the bathroom, but the door was shut. Micah leaned over to spy under the door and didn't see any light poking out. He waited a moment before speaking. His breath caught in his throat, a hangover from that terrible nightmare. The damn thing was too hard to shake.

It had felt so real, so final.

"Frank?"

No response. Maybe he'd slipped down to the snack machine for a bag of chips? With everything they had going on, Frank probably would have woken him up to let him know about that, at least. It wasn't like Frank to leave unannounced, and then not to check in.

Micah dialed Frank. Held the phone up to his ear and felt the dampness of sweat rub onto the phone.

A second later, something on top of the television vibrated.

Frank was gone, and he hadn't taken his phone with him.

## CHAPTER NINETEEN

F RANK FIRST NOTICED a stinging in the side of his neck, before he could open his eyes. Like that pulse of pain after a shot at the doctor's office. His head felt woozy, heavy. Mouth thick, an ache running up and down his spine.

He'd been drugged. Syringe to the neck. He could tell that much right away. His hand hurt, probably from punching that casino bouncer in the face. And finally, the same pain from yesterday still burned at his side. As far as the usual catalog of aches and pains that troubled Frank on a daily basis, this was a little above the norm.

When he opened his eyes, he immediately recognized that he was in a motel room, but not the same room in which he'd gone to sleep last night. Not the same motel, either. These walls were blue, and not brown like the room he'd been sharing with Micah.

Micah wasn't here. Some other man sat in a chair at the end of the bed. White guy.

"Hello," the man said. East coast accent.

Frank sat up, a little surprised he wasn't tied to the bed. Had a flash of memory of waking up after a blackout drunk, more than thirty years ago. He'd started drinking in Chicago and ended up in Detroit, in a motel room a bit like this one. His wallet missing and a dislocated shoulder. That had been one mysterious bender he'd never fully pieced together.

Now, Frank noticed the pistol in the man's hands, topped with a noise suppressor. The gun was pointed at the ground, but the man's finger was hovering above the trigger.

"You must be confused," the man said. "Wondering why you're waking up in a strange motel room with a strange guy staring at you."

Frank's throat was dry. His head was slow and full of wobbly jelly. He hated to feel intoxicated, because he'd given up the drinking and drugs over twenty years ago and hadn't ever wanted to feel that way again. He wouldn't feel this way by choice.

"I'm not confused at all. I have a pretty good idea why I'm here."

The man tilted his head. "Oh? You might be surprised."

"Try me," Frank said. This guy had to be part of the casino Crossroads gang, or possibly cartel. There weren't too many other options. Frank didn't have any other enemies that weren't already dead or in jail. At least, none that he could think of right now.

The man sighed. "You flew into the Bishop airport three days ago on Southwest Airlines. You had a ginger ale on the plane."

Frank didn't feel intimidated by how much this guy knew, because he'd seen this tactic before. But it had probably eliminated the cartel possibility. He couldn't imagine a scenario where the cartel would go to any length to find out his beverage choice. This kind of thing was more mafia style: *we know who you are, we know where your children go to school, now tell us what we want to know.*

"Yeah, but what *kind* of ginger ale did I order?"

The man grinned and wagged a finger at him. "What are you doing in Michigan, Frank?"

"I used to live here. It's not a state secret."

"Come back to see all the sights?"

"I was a cop in this city for a long time," Frank said, putting emphasis on the word *cop*. Not that it would probably scare his captor, but Frank figured the guy should, at least, know who he was about to kill. You could still get the death penalty for killing a retired cop.

Frank tried to survey the room without moving his head too much, only using his peripheral vision. In the bed, he wouldn't be able to get up and reach the door before this guy could put a bullet in him. His best hope was that the man would try to move him to some other place, and that's when Frank would go for the gun.

A hand-to-hand scramble might get iffy, though, with

whatever they'd given him still slowing his reaction time.

"I know what you used to do for a living," the man said. "And I know all about your bail bondsman *slash* bounty hunter business in Denver. How does that work, by the way? Usually, those are two separate entities. Don't bail bondsmen hire bail recovery agents when their clients fail to show up for court?"

"I'm licensed in Colorado. My documents are fully on the public record. I also have an assistant who works for me as a skip tracer. It's all legit and above-board."

The man frowned as if he didn't get it. Frank was about to launch into the speech about cutting out the middle man when a knock came at the door, then a pause, then three more quick knocks.

"Come in," the man said, not taking his eyes off Frank.

In stepped a woman holding a can of Faygo soda in one hand and a bag of potato chips in the other. She flicked on the lights. Attractive woman, flaming red hair and green eyes. She had the kind of statuesque figure Frank remembered actresses having in the movies he used to watch as a kid. Not like all the unkempt women in Hollywood today with their tattoos and stick-thin waists.

There was something familiar about her, but Frank couldn't place it.

The woman held out the soda. "I had to guess what you'd like, but I know you don't drink alcohol, right?"

He nodded. Then, like a slap across the face, it came to him.

"I'm gonna pass on the Faygo, but thanks anyway. Your

name is Olivia, correct? Or, at least, that's what you told my colleague your name is."

She tried to play it off, but her eyebrows did raise a fraction of an inch. Then a slight frame of a scowl lined her mouth. This pretty young woman didn't like not having the upper hand at all times.

"You two know who I am," Frank said, "so it's only fair, right?"

Olivia tilted her head at the man with the gun. "Sure, Frank, we can do it that way. The man babysitting you is named Jeremy."

Jeremy appeared unfazed.

"So," she said, "now that we all know each other, there's not much point in playing games. We'll get right down to it, then."

Frank felt his pulse rise as the pain in his side intensified. "Wait a second. I've been down this road before, and I think I can save you some time. You're going to ask me questions, and I'm going to give you answers. If you're going to kill me no matter what I say, you might as well tell me now."

Needles of anxiety pricked his chest as Olivia and Jeremy shared a look. Silence bloomed in the room for several seconds.

"Frank," Olivia finally said. "I don't know who you think we are, but we're not monsters. We debated back and forth for hours about whether or not we should even speak with you."

Looking at the two of them, they didn't seem like gangsters. And Frank had already ruled out cartel. That left only one option. "No, not monsters, I would suspect. Are you feds?"

She spread a flat and annoyed smile. "We're not that kind of monster, either. We're not beholden to a lot of the rules those guys have to follow when working in an official capacity. We're private contractors, out on loan to some important people who you don't need to know about."

Frank wondered if they might know his sister Anita. Probably not, but it would be worth a phone call. If he left this room alive, anyway. "The almost-plane-crash that you were in with Micah. Did you somehow orchestrate that?"

Both Olivia and Jeremy burst out laughing. "Good God, no. I'm not a wizard, Frank. That was just dumb luck. Didn't hurt establishing a rapport with Micah, though." She paused to sigh. "Not that it did me any good because now you know my face, so there's not much chance of cozying up to him again. That was probably a pointless road to travel, to begin with."

"So you're not planning on killing me."

Olivia pursed her lips. "I haven't decided yet. That depends on how our conversation goes."

They wanted to keep him unsure and scared. Frank knew she already had decided what to do with him, but making it seem like his future was up for discussion would instill a twinge of hope in him. Make him want to cooperate to ensure his survival.

Jeremy passed the gun from one hand to the other.

"Micah dropped out of Witness Protection some time

ago," Jeremy said. "Do you know why?"

"He didn't think they had anything else to offer him. Thought he could do a better job of protecting himself on his own, and he didn't like having to check in with his handlers."

Olivia ran a finger along the length of one eyebrow, stroking it. "And they let him do that?"

"Sure," Frank said. "They couldn't force him to stay. He served his time and had no official parole."

Jeremy cleared his throat. "And what has he been doing since he started protecting himself on his own?"

"What do you mean?"

"We know he officially works for you," Olivia said, "but does he do anything on the side? Maybe some freelance work for Tyson Darby?"

"Darby? The guy who owns the strip club? What the hell are you talking about?"

"We're just trying to close those loops."

Frank had a hard time believing this line of questioning. It didn't make any sense. "Hell no, he doesn't do any work for Tyson Darby."

Olivia leaned against the wardrobe, exchanged another look with Jeremy. "Any kind of illegal activity at all?"

"No," Frank said. "What are you getting at?"

"We know how he made his living before he entered Witness Protection. And we know how dangerous he is."

Frank bit back a smirk. These people—private military or whatever they were—learned all about Micah from some government file. Thought they knew him.

"Micah isn't like that anymore. He's not the same person. Seems like you're going to an awful lot of trouble to look into him, when you could just tap his phone or whatever the hell else you people do."

Olivia and Jeremy shared another look. Something else was going on here, and Frank could tell. Whatever it was, they weren't going to spill it.

"Look," Frank said, "I don't know what you want with Micah. But he is not at all involved in his old business, I can practically guarantee you that. Why would he be? Most of them think he's dead, and the ones who think he might still be alive put out a price on his head. Micah Reed is not interested in gangster business. He's interested in keeping a low profile and fading into obscurity."

"If that's true," Olivia said, "then why are the two of you here in Michigan? Why are you visiting plastic surgeons who happen to turn up dead right within minutes after talking to you?"

"Oh, we already discussed that," Jeremy said, "while you were out getting the soda. They're here to see the sights. Right, Frank?"

"What we're doing is none of your concern. You wanted to know if Micah is involved with his old people, and I'm telling you he's not. There ain't shit else to say about it."

Olivia put a hand to her face and tugged at her lower lip. Chest slightly expanding and falling, her eyes narrowing at Frank.

CHAPTER TWENTY

THE MORNING SUN pierced through the break in the motel room curtains, slowly shifting a patch of light across the bedspread. Micah searched Frank's phone, trying to think of who he could call. He almost dialed Anita Mueller but didn't know how she would be able to help.

He dropped Frank's phone and rubbed his face. Probably, Micah's boss had gone out in the middle of the night to get a soda or something, and had been snatched. And given the way Frank had burst from the back door of the mall yesterday, it made sense someone from the Crossroads gang had located them and kidnapped him. They'd only seen Frank, not Micah.

He had no choice but to return to the Dort Mall and get access to that casino. They might recognize him and they might not, but Micah had nowhere else to look. He couldn't sit around here and wait for Frank's lifeless body to be flung from the back of a car as it sped past the motel.

He left Frank's phone on top of the television and grabbed the rental car keys. The thickness of the springtime humidity greeted him as he opened the door and stepped into the air. Denver was like the surface of the moon compared to Michigan.

He raced across town and connected with the Dort Highway to reach the mall. As he came near it, a fast food place caught his eye. Big John Steak and Onion. Must have been a local spot, because he'd never heard of it before.

Through the restaurant's glass window, he spotted the three guys from the day before. Rourke, the big guy Ethan, and the long-haired blond one whose name Micah hadn't caught. The three of them, sitting at a booth inside, holding sandwiches in front of their faces.

Maybe they all lived in this neighborhood, this wasteland of shady porno shops and gentlemen's clubs. Maybe they were big steak and onion fans. Either way, whatever they wanted with this mall had nothing to do with Micah.

He drove into the parking lot and wasted a little time thinking about where to park. There was an exit to the casino leading out from the back of the mall, but entering that way would probably expose him too quickly. He needed to be inconspicuous if he wanted to learn anything.

Had Frank said how to access the casino from inside? If he had, Micah didn't remember.

He parked on the front side of the mall and palmed the steering wheel, watching that pale ruffled awning sway in the breeze. He felt the nub of Boba Fett in his pocket, ran his fingers back and forth across it.

"Don't know what we're going to find in there, Boba."

Boba Fett said nothing.

Micah ran a hand over his stubbly head, pushed the glasses up his nose, and left the car. When he pulled back one of the glass doors to enter the mall, he was immediately struck by the immense amount of crap everywhere. Hundreds of things were hanging on the walls, suspended from the ceiling, standing out in the open. Sports equipment, street signs, wooden statues. It was like the inside of some pawn shop owner's garage.

"Holy crap, what is this place?" Micah said to no one. Literally no one, because he seemed to be the only person in the open area of this shopping mall. There was a little fast food joint to his right, but every other shopping space seemed to be closed.

Some voices echoed down the hall to his left, so he headed that way. A thin layer of dust coated the floor. Did no one even sweep?

A set of stairs in the middle of the wide hallway led down, so he followed them, but the door at the bottom was boarded up. No basement access that way. He thought about yanking the boards off and busting through the door, but that wouldn't be inconspicuous, either.

The voices led him back up the stairs and to the end of the hallway, where he found one business actually open, a hockey sporting goods store. The red wheel-and-wings logo of the Detroit Red Wings everywhere. Lights on, employees walking around normally as if the rest of the mall weren't on life support.

Micah entered the store and a kid in a polo shirt with a lanyard around his neck jogged up to him.

"Morning, sir. Can I help you?"

Micah had to make a quick decision. He had no idea how to find this entrance to the casino on his own, and maybe these employees knew about it. Maybe this hockey business was some front to keep the cops at bay.

"I'm looking for something you can't find in the store."

The kid raised an eyebrow and chirped an uncomfortable laugh. "Do you mean you want us to order something? We have a pretty big selection, maybe you should look around first."

"No. I'm not looking to buy something. I'm looking to win something, if you know what I mean."

The kid's brow continued to crease further, and Micah started to think this had been a terrible idea. Maybe they *didn't* know about the casino downstairs, as weird as that seemed.

"I'm not sure I understand," the kid said.

"Yeah, I can see you don't. Sorry to be all weird and cryptic. It's just... is there someone else I can talk to, maybe someone who's worked here for a long time?"

The kid frowned, then looked at the back and waved someone over. A man with a salt and pepper beard approached, and then shooed the kid away.

"Can I help you, sir?" the bearded man said. He had suspicion etched in the lines of his face.

"Yes. I'm looking for something you keep in the basement. Do you know what I'm talking about?"

The man's expression fell. "You need to be a little more specific, sir. And I need to know who told you about what it is you're asking for."

Micah struggled to remember the name Frank had said, the guy who runs the casino. Harry? Henry?

Harvey.

"Harvey sent me," Micah said. "I'm just looking to have some fun."

"Are you with law enforcement?"

Funny how people asked that question and expected an honest response. Maybe because of the television myth that cops were compelled to identify themselves when asked. Like they had some contractual code of truth they'd agreed to live by. *Curses. You've foiled my undercover operation because you were smart enough to ask, so now I have to tell you.*

Micah shook his head.

The bearded man pursed his lips, breathing in and out as soft pop music warbled from unseen speakers. Eventually, he nodded. "Okay, sir. After me, please."

Micah's shoulders fell as the tension bled out of him. He followed the bearded man to the back of the store and into a gigantic office room. More random Americana piled everywhere in here, too.

The man pointed to a door in the back. "Right that way, sir."

# CHAPTER TWENTY-ONE

THE EMPLOYEE DISAPPEARED back into the main store and shut the door behind him. Micah approached the door on the far side, his heart thudding against his rib cage. Trouble swallowing. He didn't have much of a plan. Get in, find Frank, and then get out. But how? He didn't have a gun, and he hadn't brought anything else to use as a weapon, because he had to assume they would search him.

If Frank was being held in a back room somewhere, how would Micah access it? This was a casino, so they would obviously have lots of eyes everywhere.

Micah would have to figure something out in real time. If Frank died, then nothing else would matter. They had to reunite so they could get on with the business of figuring out who killed the lookalike and why. And also, so he could stop kicking himself for letting his mentor be kidnapped in the middle of the night.

He had to do *something*.

His tennis shoes made no sound descending the stairs, and then he turned at the bottom to find a man sitting at a desk. Older, gray hair, broad chest and a solid wall of belly. Bushy eyebrows, like slugs hovering above his pupils. Looked like one of those old mafia tough guys.

The tough bushy-eyebrowed guy stood, and Micah could see the bulge of a gun underneath his suit coat.

"Are you lost?"

A self-conscious fear gripped him. Micah was wearing the fake contacts and glasses, but if his face sparked any amount of recognition, it wouldn't take long for them to piece the rest together.

"No, I know where I am. Feeling lucky, wanted to turn that into more luck."

"Do you mind if I ask how much money you have with you?"

"Um, sure," Micah said as he reached for his wallet. Bushy Eyebrows flinched as Micah's hand moved behind him, and Micah held up his free hand to show he meant no harm. "Just getting my cash."

"Of course, sir."

Micah pulled it out, not sure what he was going to find inside. The wallet answered back: two twenties and a few spare singles. He didn't think that was quite enough to qualify him as a high roller.

"I'm mostly checking it out today," he said as he flashed forty-three dollars at Bushy Eyebrows. "Some friends of mine and I are looking for a new spot since our last one went under."

"And where was your old spot, sir?"

Micah cursed himself under his breath. Should have known the guy would ask that. "Not around here. Back in Denver. My friends and I are in town for a few weeks, and we need something fun to pass the time."

The bouncer lifted his sleeve to his lips and whispered, then he tapped against a Bluetooth sticking from his ear. Nodded.

"Okay, sir, the password today is *counterfeit*."

Micah almost laughed. Counterfeit, like the man lying on a slab, the one who had Micah's same face. Had to be a coincidence, didn't it? Or had this man already figured out who Micah looked like?

"Got it," he said as Bushy Eyebrows stepped aside and motioned to the door. Micah didn't give him another look as he proceeded beyond the tough guy and met the second level bouncer, who eyed him and asked for the password, then searched him before letting him pass through yet another door. The real casino was on the other side.

A wave of tobacco smoke made Micah's eyes burn as soon as he entered the main room. Smelled like the musty brown stench of cigars. At least, the lights in the casino were so low that it didn't seem like anyone would see his face.

Neither of the bouncers had looked at him with raised eyebrows, so perhaps they weren't involved in the looka-like's murder. Or maybe these people had never had anything to do with it. Micah was only here to find his boss, and anything else was secondary.

He took stock of the room. He didn't care about the roulette tables or poker tables, the blinking lights of the slot machines, or the women escorting trays full of drinks. His eyes were on the walls and any doors he would find there. If Frank were here, he'd be in a back office somewhere.

A dozen men in suits with coils sprouting from their ears lined the walls and milled throughout the forty or fifty people gambling in clumps at various tables. Aside from the mechanical sounds of the slots and some chatter from the card dealers, it was relatively quiet. No music came from overhead speakers.

A young woman with bright blue eyes appeared out of nowhere, pushing a set of barely-contained fake breasts in Micah's face. "What can I get you, hon?"

Micah had had plenty of experience saying no to alcohol in the seven months he'd been sober, and it was getting a little easier every time. Still made his mouth water, though. He still wished he could get angry at the girl for tempting him, but she didn't know any better.

"Nothing for me."

"You sure, hon? It's on the house."

"I'm sure. Thank you, though."

She shrugged and left him, then Micah started to plan how he was going to slip near the outskirts of the room to investigate. All the gamblers in the room were at the tables or the slots, which were clustered in the center of the room. No one was hanging out on the fringes. Most of the wall area was shrouded in darkness. But Micah knew he couldn't just walk the length of the room with impunity, trying to open locked doors. Someone would notice.

His best bet would be to try to make it look like he was surveying the tables, trying to discern which one was his best chance to make money. If they questioned him, that's what he would say.

The room was spacious. It appeared to run most of the length of the mall. It might take him a couple minutes to circle all the way around. He started at an illuminated area with a cashier behind a locked cage, and he asked for twenty bucks worth of chips.

The middle-aged woman behind the counter frowned at him. "Are you sure, sir? The lowest limit at the tables is ten. Maybe you would like the quarter slots better."

"I'm just taking it all in. If I like it, I'll be back later."

She glanced over Micah's shoulder, and he resisted the urge to peak around to see what she'd been looking at. If they were on to him already, he'd have to make a hasty exit.

She handed two white chips to him, and Micah held them up, smiling at her. But he had to force the smile because he felt increasingly stupid for having come down here into this basement casino. Someone was going to question him, and soon.

When Micah turned around, he found out exactly how soon.

Before him stood a giant of a man, with shoulders that seemed wide enough to give him trouble walking through doorways. Head clean-shaven, beady eyes, and the tiny hint of a faded tattoo of a swastika just above the collar of his shirt. Prison type tattoo. Micah had seen a few of them applied in his short stint in the protective custody wing of the prison where he'd done his time.

"Hello," came the man's deep and booming voice. "Are you enjoying yourself, Mr…"

"Templeton," Micah said. "Roland Templeton."

"Well, Mr. Templeton, my name is Harvey. This is my room."

A little pause followed, and Micah realized he was supposed to say something. "Well… thank you for having me here."

"I don't mean to be rude, but something tells me you're not here to gamble."

Micah froze, didn't know what to say. And while he was thinking, he noticed Harvey flexing his giant Aryan hands, the veins on his wrists turning into rivers.

# CHAPTER TWENTY-TWO

OLIVIA OPENED THE door of the motel room as she ended her phone conversation. If she didn't have to spend so much time checking in and explaining herself to her superiors, maybe she could get some real work done. Always left a bad taste in her mouth.

Jeremy was still leaning against the dresser, gun in his hand. Frank was in the bed. His hand at his side, a grimace on his face.

"Everything okay?" Jeremy said.

"More or less," Olivia said as she set her phone and purse on top of the air conditioner. "We're good." She gave Frank a look. "What's going on with you? Why are you making that face?"

"Pain in my side, like a Doberman biting me every few seconds. Got serious a couple minutes ago."

Jeremy cleared his throat. "We didn't poison you, if that's what you're thinking."

"I didn't say that you did. But since you didn't, do you have any Pepto? Maalox?"

Olivia shook her head. "I don't think so. But you can go get your own." She stepped away from the door, leaving Frank a clear path to it. "Jeremy will drive you back to your motel. If you're ready to go, that is."

Jeremy stood and slipped his gun into a dresser drawer.

Frank chewed on his lower lip, eying the space between the bed and the door. "That's it? Even though I know who you people are, you're just going to let me go?"

"We're not bad people, Mr. Mueller," she said. "You've convinced me that Micah Reed isn't back to his old ways, and so we don't have anything further to ask you. Now that we're done here, you can get back to seeing the sights."

Jeremy forced a smile. "We appreciate your time this morning. I know we must have put a scare into you, but as one professional to another, I hope there are no hard feelings."

Frank mulled this over, then he tossed back the bedsheet and stood. The grimace on his face turned sour. He moaned and swayed on his feet, teeth clenched.

"Maybe we should skip the motel and take you to the hospital," Jeremy said.

Frank held up a hand. "No, I'm fine. Probably all those donuts I ate yesterday. Should have known better."

He gave one last glance at the both of them, still not trusting it. Olivia backed further away from the door to help him understand that she wasn't going to bum rush him when he tried to leave.

As Frank lurched to the door, Jeremy opened it for him. "I'll meet you down in front of the motel office. Give me two minutes."

Frank put his head down and then slipped out to the breezeway, and waddled down to the stairs. Jeremy watched him go.

Olivia shut the door. "What's up?"

"Do you want me to actually take Frank back to his motel?"

"Sure. I don't see any reason to kill him. I'll check out here and meet you back at our hotel in an hour."

Jeremy scrunched his face. "Then I'm not sure I understand why we bothered to pick him up. Seems like an extra variable that could complicate everything."

"Possibly, but I think it's more likely it works out to our advantage and speeds up the timeline. If Micah is clean, then we move on to phase two."

His face relaxed, realization brightening his eyes. Jeremy could be a little slow to catch on sometimes.

"Do you think Frank bought it?" he said. "Our motivations for investigating Micah, I mean. We did lay it on thick with those questions about Tyson Darby. Seemed like a bit of a reach to be so curious about his criminal past."

Olivia hitched her purse over her shoulder and checked to make sure the safety on her pistol was engaged. "It doesn't matter what he believes. We need to keep in mind two things." She held up a finger. "What we're doing here is important. When it's all said and done, our actions are going to save lives."

She held up a second finger. "And Frank or Micah knowing who we are doesn't change anything. We were going to have to interact with them at some point, so from that perspective, nothing has changed. We're still going to ensure the chain of events stays pure, and if those two are there when it happens, that's fine too."

"I understand."

Olivia sat on the bed and crossed her legs, ensuring she had Jeremy's attention. "But we need to be wary. If they do get in the way, we won't let them become a problem."

# CHAPTER TWENTY-THREE

MICAH STOOD TALL, didn't let his shoulders slump or roll forward. "I've told you people twice already," he said to the big casino owner Harvey, "I'm here checking it out. I might come back later with some friends and spend more time, but I'm only looking to get a feel of the place today."

The air changed, and Micah knew that at least two people were now standing behind him. Harvey didn't look over Micah's shoulder, but he didn't have to. Micah felt their proximity.

The claustrophobia surrounded him. Not quite as intense as being strapped into an airplane seat, but the feeling indicated he wasn't in control over the space around him. A flush came to his cheeks and his chest tightened. He didn't like being enclosed.

Micah lowered on his haunches an inch or two, just enough to prepare himself to run if a hand gripped his

shoulder. He didn't want to flee since Frank was still missing. Also, Frank had already used up his one chance to
investigate the casino. Wouldn't do much good if Micah
also imploded that bridge.

The slot machines blinked and clinked and made their
cartoony sounds all around, but the little patch of carpet
Micah and Harvey were standing on seemed as quiet as a
church. Harvey breathed, didn't say anything.

Out of the corner of his eye, Micah noticed the pretty
blue-eyed girl who'd tried to serve him drinks. She
clutched an empty drink tray to her chest, her face full of
fear. Maybe she'd seen her share of people come into the
casino through the door and leave in the trunk of a car.
The worry lines etched into her forehead suggested she
thought the same would happen to Micah.

He wanted to wink at her, to say *hey, it's okay, I know
what I'm doing.* But before he could, she lowered the tray
and strode back through a set of swinging doors. Gawking
too long would probably get her in trouble. How did this
ratty underground casino recruit pretty women like that to
come work here? What could they have to offer?

Then, Micah remembered how Frank said that Crossroads dabbled in prostitution. He didn't want to think
about that. Didn't want to picture the waitress taking her
clothes off for money.

After the longest pause in history, Harvey slipped
meaty hands into his pockets and sucked through his teeth.
"Okay then, Mr. Templeton. Have a good time."

Micah tried not to make it obvious his breath was

exhaling in a shudder. Harvey and the men standing behind Micah dispersed. He stood unmolested in the dimly lit, smoke-filled room. Only one anonymous gambler among three or four dozen others, hoping to turn cash into more cash.

He wiped his sweaty hands on his jeans and picked a direction, toward a blackjack table. Approached a chair next to two older men, opposite a dealer in a slick white three-piece suit. The dealer wore a smirk, his hands clasped behind his back.

"Hello, sir. Is your phone off?"

"Yes," Micah said.

"Then have a seat at the table."

Micah sat and threw down one of his two chips. An image of Olivia popped into his head, her long red hair like coils of satin. He wondered if she'd been thinking about him, puzzling over why he hadn't called yet. Maybe he would call her later, engage in some small talk. But then he'd have to lie to her about where he was, or lie about why he was in Michigan, and Micah was tired of lying. Tired of perpetuating the same fake backstory to all the new acquaintances in his life. Something close to the truth, in which he would say he grew up in Oklahoma, but would conveniently leave out the parts about dropping out of college, stumbling into the employ of Luis Velasquez and the American branch of the Sinaloa cartel. Leave out the violence he'd committed during his time there, his arrest and participation in Witness Protection. Leave out going to prison and reinventing himself in Colorado with a new name and a new profession.

The true story of his life didn't make for a good conversation topic, since Micah still had living family members who would be at risk if anyone uncovered his old identity.

The dealer dropped two cards in front of him, but Micah barely noticed. His eyes were tracking Harvey as he ducked into a door at the far corner marked *maintenance*. Not *manager's office*. Why would Harvey disappear into a maintenance closet?

That had to be where they were keeping Frank.

"Sir?" the dealer said.

Micah looked down at his cards. A king and a queen. He tried to remember the hand motion that meant *stay*, but couldn't. He hadn't ever been much of a gambler, had never understood the adrenaline rush that made some people lose themselves in it. An ironic mystery. Alcohol had thoroughly conquered him for so many years, but gambling—something as equally as addictive for others— had never hooked him.

"Sir?"

The two other gamblers at the table were starting to grow annoyed. One of the older men was chewing on a drinking straw. The mangled piece of plastic danced as he swished it around his mouth.

"Sorry. Stay."

"Very well, sir." The dealer flipped over his cards. A jack and an ace. The two older men at the table groaned, but

Micah didn't bother. He got up and walked away from the table, on a path toward that maintenance door.

He weaved through a group of four men who were all stumbling drunk, trying to count their chips. One of them was holding a stein of beer, and a bit sloshed onto Micah's leg. The drunk mumbled a bleary apology and Micah ignored him.

Back when Micah was drinking, he'd had a habit of spilling alcohol on himself. Now it seemed, other people did it for him.

The door was in sight, but a couple of casino guards stood on either side of it. His brain sped through options about how to lure them away from that door without starting a fight.

He didn't get very far into the thought process.

Still twenty paces away, someone appeared before him. A familiar man, and it only took Micah a second to recognize him as one of the two assailants he'd seen fleeing the scene of the plastic surgeon's murder. The man Frank had identified.

He slipped a hand into his coat pocket and shifted a toothpick from one side of his mouth to the other. "Where the hell do you think you're going?"

# CHAPTER TWENTY-FOUR

MICAH HALF-WALKED, half-stumbled out of the Dort Mall as he was half-escorted, half-thrown out. The man who was pushing him along the barren interior of the mall didn't say a word. Micah thought of a dozen snappy one-liners to whip out, but didn't see the benefit.

The guy opened the door and gave Micah one last heave, sending him a couple feet into the parking lot. With a sneer, he shut the door behind him. Micah could have easily snatched the man by the hand and used his momentum to flip him onto the ground, but what would be the point?

Micah had gotten off easy. They hadn't recognized him as being the same as the lookalike they'd killed. Or at least, they hadn't let on if they had recognized him. But why *wouldn't* they have recognized him? Even with the fake blue eyes and shaved head, it should have been obvious.

Micah fished his phone out of his pocket and powered it on. A text message from Frank appeared.

I'm okay. Back at HQ.

Micah jumped in his car and raced to the motel. He was only a couple miles away, so he didn't bother calling first. The knowledge that Frank was still alive, and not dead in a dumpster somewhere made him feel less stupid about his pointless venture into the belly of the mall.

Micah paused in the parking lot before leaving the rental.

There was something strange about the lot at the motel. Something different. He ignored this bit of weird intuition as he headed for the exterior stairs and ran to the second floor. Jogged down the concrete breezeway, slapping the metal railing for balance.

When he opened the door to the room, he found it empty.

"Frank?"

"Back here, kid," came a voice from the bathroom. A moment later, Frank emerged, dabbing the corner of his mouth with a hand towel. His eyes were drooping, his skin tinged with green.

"Frank, you look like shit."

The old man grinned, a sour crease to his lips. "Yeah." He sniffed the air.

"That's me you're smelling. Some jerk spilled beer on me today."

Frank leaned against the wall for support. "I hate it when they do that."

"What happened to you?"

"Food poisoning, I think. My stomach is in knots."

Micah hustled to him and helped Frank get into bed. The old man groaned as he reclined.

"Where did you go last night?"

"I was kidnapped. They came right into the room and snatched me. Pumped me full of something, maybe that interacted with whatever I ate."

A pang of guilt throttled Micah. He should have known Frank was being taken, but he'd been too busy with his paranoid dreams about a plane crash. Too busy thinking about himself, as usual.

"Who snatched you?"

"Olivia."

Micah sucked air into his lungs, but still found himself short of breath. The room seemed to shrink to the size of a closet. Frank couldn't have said *Olivia*.

"My Olivia? With the green eyes and the red hair?"

Frank nodded. "That's the one. But I don't think she's really your Olivia."

Micah's head spun as he sank onto the bed next to Frank. He didn't know how to process such a bombshell. But Frank wouldn't lie about something like this, and besides, Micah was reasonably sure he'd never said Olivia's name to Frank before.

"She and her partner are government contractors. They

didn't say, but private military would be my guess. I checked with Anita and she'd never heard of them."

"What did they want?"

"They wanted to know if you were involved in any gangster business. They heard about the lookalike in the morgue and thought maybe you'd faked your own death so you could start up a criminal enterprise or something."

Micah paced around the room, tapping a finger against his temple. The shock was already wearing off, and Micah carefully considered Frank's words. It made sense. Olivia had been on the flight so she could verify it wasn't him on that slab in Flint, The whole thing had been a sham.

"This is crazy," Micah said. "After all that? Damn. I liked her."

"Them's the breaks, kid."

Micah realized he was standing in the middle of the room, so he took a seat next to the bed. "Do we need to be worried about her?"

"I don't know. Maybe, maybe not. She and her partner said they're satisfied, but that doesn't mean anything. I can expect they'll be watching us, at the least."

Micah recalled their conversation on the flight, about why she'd been in Fresno. Now that he thought about it, her responses had sounded rehearsed.

"What did you do with yourself this morning?" Frank said.

"I went back to the casino."

"That explains the spilled beer. Learn anything interesting?"

"Not really. I was looking for you. I saw your guy Harvey and the guy who killed our plastic surgeon. There's something wrong going on there, Frank, I know it."

Frank moaned and put a hand on his side. "I don't doubt that."

"Do we need to get you to the hospital?"

"I'll be fine," Frank said as he waved a dismissive hand. "I need some rest, that's all."

He didn't look fine, but Micah wasn't going to force him to go. No one spoke for a moment, and Micah felt a sudden darkness. Doubt wrapped its arms around him like a hug from an overbearing aunt.

"Frank, I'm not sure what we're doing here anymore."

Frank pushed himself back onto the pillows, grimacing as he did so.

"Maybe you're looking at it the wrong way."

"How should I look at it?"

Frank sighed. "You spent a year in prison?"

"Almost. Eleven months in Ohio."

"So you've seen how people act when they're locked up. When they lose everything. How, when the color of their skin is the only thing they can claim as their own, they split off into natural groups divided by it."

Micah shrugged. "It was a little like that, yeah. But I was in a protective custody wing, so it wasn't quite like gcnpop. Most of us had the bond of being snitches, which was a pretty exclusive group. But I don't get what this has to do with our current situation."

Frank nodded and clucked his teeth a few times,

collecting himself. "Harvey's gang isn't like a regular drugs and numbers operation. They're driven by something much deeper than the love of money and power. They're driven by a need to purify the world. It gets to me like nothing else does. Makes me feel powerless and full of resentment, in a way I can't describe."

Frank didn't usually open up like this about his feelings. He and Micah talked about sobriety and their concepts of a higher power all the time, but never about politics or race or religion.

"You asked me what we're doing here," Frank said. "I would have come back here to confront Harvey someday, morgue John Doe or not. It was time for me to face up to this resentment I've been carrying around."

Frank's sudden revelation made Micah feel like he needed to do the same. The secret that had been tugging at his insides. Something he'd been carrying around for a long time, but hadn't ever been able to bring himself to mention to Frank.

His lips formed the words, and he couldn't believe what he was about to say. But the words tumbled out anyway.

"The first person I ever killed was a cop," Micah said. "I don't think I told you that before."

Frank adopted a grave look as he shook his head. "You haven't."

"I'd done lots of terrible things in the cartel before. I've put people in the hospital and I was usually too drunk to know how wrong it was. But the cop, he was my first. It was self-defense, but no one else would have seen it that way."

Frank's eyes fell to the bedspread. Micah didn't know how Frank would take the news, since Frank himself had been a cop for decades. Even though the old man was his closest friend, that's not the kind of thing he might shrug off.

"I was in a situation," Micah said, "and I didn't have any other choice. Is that like the powerlessness you were talking about before?"

"Not really. But it doesn't matter. The things you did when you were drinking... that's the old you. The abandoned person you don't have to be anymore, as long as you stay sober."

Micah felt the grip of shame squeeze him. He knew that the drunken cop-killing person was his past, but it still felt so raw and fresh. He decided to change the subject.

"What happened down there in the casino, Frank?"

"When I went in, I didn't know if I'd make it back out. But I had to see it for myself. Had to see if that evil still thrived after all these years."

"And what did you find?"

Frank laughed, a wet and gurgling sound. "Nothing so bold and earth-shattering. Facing up to my own resentment turned out to be anti-climactic. I got into a scuffle with a bouncer as soon as I got in there, and I made a break for it. It was either that or shoot up the place. I chose to run."

Micah let out a slow, labored exhalation. "And we're

right where we started, with nothing. Nowhere closer to finding out who that John Doe in the morgue was, or how to prove who killed him."

"So, we're stuck. What do you have in mind for our next move?"

Micah didn't know. They could turn everything over to the cops and go home, and that seemed like the smartest plan. Remove themselves from the whole messed-up equation. But somehow, doing that didn't seem right. Seemed like failure. He couldn't walk away, not when these people had made it so personal to him. There had to be a way to reveal who this lookalike was.

As he was considering his options, Frank groaned and gripped his side. His face became a twisted portrait of pain.

Micah stood up. "Okay, we're taking you to the hospital."

For once, Frank didn't fight him. "Okay, yeah, maybe we should go. It's getting worse."

He helped Frank get out of bed and lifted the old man to his feet. Gathered up his phone and supported Frank on the way across the carpet.

When Micah threw back the door, a bullet whizzed past his head.

# CHAPTER TWENTY-FIVE

R OURKE SAT BEHIND the wheel, engine humming. He passed a baseball back and forth between his hands, squeezing it too hard with each toss. His palms ached from the grip.

The car was parked on the unused bridge over Saginaw Street, among the collection of fast food packaging and hypodermic needles. On a slab of concrete where junkies came to lose themselves, where lonely men came to get blowjobs from sick hookers while they watched the cars thunder along the road below.

Carter sat beside him in the passenger seat and Ethan was in the back. Carter was texting, his fingers flying over the phone keyboard at warp speed. Ethan had his earbuds in, bopping his head to some music. Rap, probably, because that was all the kid would listen to.

"Ethan," Rourke said, trying to catch his eye in the rearview.

Ethan took out his earbuds. "What?"

"We've been sitting here too long. Is your guy usually on time?"

"First of all," Ethan said, "this isn't my guy. It's not like I know him or anything. You guys got to understand that he's a friend of a friend of some Yooper named Scully that I barely know who goes to my gym. If makes him *my guy*, then sure. So I don't know, is the answer to your question."

Rourke flared his nostrils and squeezed the baseball in one hand so hard that pain shot up his elbow. Ethan slipped his earbuds back in and resumed bopping his head.

"Hey," Carter said, smacking Rourke on the shoulder. "You need to relax, dude. Your worrying is only going to put the finishing touches on that ulcer you've been grooming. All the contingencies are accounted for."

"I don't even know what that means," Rourke said.

Ethan took his earbuds out again, oblivious. "We should go get some food after this."

Carter popped the glove box and took out a pistol. He checked the clip and tested the safety. "We're just buying some assault rifles from some guy we don't know. What could possibly go wrong?"

Despite the tension, Rourke chuckled a little. They were running out of time to raid the casino, and he knew it. If this weapons dealer didn't show up, they were in serious trouble. Even though Rourke himself had insisted on setting a hard date to get it done, now he doubted if their plan had legs.

"Seriously," Carter said, "why are you so agitated?"

"Fair question," Rourke said. He didn't want his two friends to know how uncertain he felt about everything. What good would that do for their leader to show his weakness?

Headlights flashed among the trees at the other end of the bridge.

"Oh, thank Christ," Rourke said. "He's here."

Carter shoved the magazine into the pistol and pushed his glasses up his nose as a big truck came into view. "Except why are there four of them?"

Ethan paused his music and leaned forward, placing his fleshy hands on the headrests of the seats in front. "Great. Mexicans."

"What's wrong with Mexicans?" Rourke said.

Ethan grumbled. "These don't look the like mow-your-lawn kind of Mexicans. More like the put-you-in-a-flaming-stack-of-tires kind."

"Damn, Ethan," Carter said. "For someone who donates to the Anti-Defamation League, you're pretty racist."

"Not the same thing," Ethan said.

"Guys. Stop it," Rourke said. "This might turn ugly. There are two more heaters under the seats, but please don't walk out there with your guns raised. One Mexican, four Mexicans, it doesn't matter. We need what these guys are selling, and I don't want to spook them."

Ethan ducked and got the two revolvers, then offered one to Rourke.

"You remember that piece-of-shit guy from Madison

who shorted us on that bag of hydroponic last year?" Ethan said.

Rourke remembered. "Of course. And I know what you're getting at. This isn't that same kind of situation. I don't think you'll get the chance to throw anyone off a second-story balcony today."

The truck rolled slowly toward them, crushing beer cans under oversized tires. The four men inside were stone-faced.

Ethan pointed at the railing of the bridge, at the cars rolling by underneath. "We'll see how it goes."

"Let's try not to start shooting if we can help it, okay?" Rourke said.

"No promises," Ethan said as he slipped the gun into his waistband and got out of the car.

"Christ on a cross," Rourke said. Ethan could be so damn impulsive. He stowed the gun in his pocket and followed Ethan out of the car. Rourke held up a hand to keep them back. He, Carter, and Ethan all sat on the hood. When Ethan sat, the car dipped a few inches.

"Be cool," Rourke said. "Please."

"I will if they will," Ethan said.

The truck stopped a couple hundred feet away on the other side of the bridge. Four truck doors opened and four men got out. All of them wearing white headbands and identical button-down shirts and khakis. Maybe a gang thing, or an insane barber shop quartet.

"Ethan," Rourke whispered, "who the hell are these guys?"

Ethan shrugged and said nothing. The four men walked in unison, like troops in battle. They kept their heads high.

"I don't like this," Carter said. Rourke agreed, but he kept his mouth shut.

The wind picked up and a discarded Halo Burger fast food bag went skittering across the bridge. A few french fries tumbled along after it.

"Which one of you is Ethan?" shouted one of the four men. In addition to his bandanna, this one had a teardrop tattoo under his eye. He stepped in front of the other three.

Ethan raised his hand. "That would be me. You're friends with Scully?"

Teardrop shook his head. "I don't know nobody named Scully. I'm just here to do some business. You're supposed to be expecting us. If you're here for something else, we going to turn around and get back in our truck."

Rourke took a couple steps forward, and two of the bandanna crew reached for guns. Rourke held up his hands in surrender. "We're here to do business, too. No need to leave. Our friend said you had three untraceable rifles plus ammunition. Is that right?"

Teardrop flicked his head at one of his associates, who jogged back to the truck. The man returned with a duffel bag, which he slung onto the ground a few feet in front of Teardrop. Teardrop then dropped to one knee and unzipped the bag. He pulled out a sleek black rifle with a wooden stock. A thing of beauty.

"AK-47," Teardrop said. "They're a little old, but they

work, no problem. You won't find anything better for this price."

Teardrop waved Rourke forward. Ethan opened his mouth, probably to protest, but Rourke held up a hand to silence his friend and then crossed the bridge. Stopped a few feet away from the duffel bag.

Up close, Rourke could see Teardrop had a spiderweb of scars crisscrossing his face, as if someone had taken a cheese grater to his cheek. The teardrop tattoo was misshapen and not completely filled in.

He grinned up at Rourke and pointed at the rifle. "These are good quality. Untraceable."

Rourke knelt. "Fifteen hundred, right? For the guns and the rounds?"

Teardrop shook his head. "Two thousand."

"Bullshit," Ethan said from behind.

Teardrop slid the gun back in the duffel and zipped it. "This is the price, my friend. If you don't want to pay the price, my people and I will go. We don't have to be here, exposing ourselves like this."

Before Rourke could respond, Ethan advanced, and so did Carter. In turn, the other three bandanna-wearers joined Teardrop. In only a few seconds, they had all gathered in the middle of the bridge.

Teardrop's crew drew their guns.

Carter and Ethan also pulled out their weapons.

Rourke rose to his feet, with his arms extended to hold back his two friends. What would they accomplish by shooting up this bridge out here today? Stupid testosterone driving everyone to act like children. "Okay, let's all be cool. We had agreed with Scully on one price, and you've said it's another. We can work this out."

"I told you," Teardrop said as he stood. "I don't know nobody named Scully. This is the price. There ain't gonna be any haggling or hemming and hawing. You've seen the merchandise, now you're going to buy it."

"Screw this," Ethan said. "This is a crock. You made us waste time coming out here and now you're trying to hustle us."

Rourke thought he might barf all over the duffel bag. He could practically feel Ethan's anger rising in pulses of energy. The big guy was likely to shoot all four of them for mouthing off, whether the deal happened or not. "Ethan, damn it, calm down."

Rourke reached in his pocket for the bank envelope. He counted his bills and held them out. "All I have is eighteen hundred."

Teardrop looked at Carter and Ethan. "What about you two? Have two hundred to pitch in?"

"Eat shit," Ethan said, and Rourke was surprised when Teardrop smiled at this.

Teardrop stared at the money, then slipped his hands into his pockets. "Okay, then. Eighteen will work. We can make this trade, then my friends and I are going to leave. If these guns ever come back on us, we will hunt down and kill each and every single person you know."

# CHAPTER TWENTY-SIX

**A** SPLIT SECOND after the bullet sliced the air next to Micah's head, he slammed the motel room door closed. Swinging the door put his upper body off balance, and with Frank's weight pulling him down, they both tumbled backward, landing on the bed.

Another bullet hit the front door of the room but didn't penetrate it. The wood splintered, just below the peephole. Bits of wood dust hung in the air.

"Can you stand?" Micah asked Frank.

"I think so," Frank said as he rolled over onto his elbows. He pressed against the bed and tried to steady himself on his feet. "There's no back door to this room. We can't stay in here."

Micah crept to the window and peeled back the edge of the curtain, but could only see a thin sliver of the parking lot. A few cars, but no people. The two wings of the motel bordered the parking lot on two sides like a steel square ruler. A third side of the parking lot exited to the street, and the fourth backed up to a fence and some trees. The motel itself stood three stories, with exterior walkways and enclosed stairs at the end of each wing. If they could get out of this room, they'd have a chance.

Micah angled his head to look at the other wing of the motel, but couldn't discern anything useful. The shots had seemed like they'd come from the parking lot, but he couldn't survey enough of it to be sure.

Another gunshot cracked the window a foot from Micah's head. He spun around, and Frank was leaning against the bed, barely upright. His food poisoning was going to make moving him around a challenge. Frank's eyes were slits and his chest heaved in time with his noticeable breathing.

"Can you walk?" Micah said.

"Looks like I don't have much choice." His voice sounded even more grumbly than usual.

Micah's thoughts raced. He tried his best to settle himself and work through it, but the bullets occasionally pelting the room didn't help. The only way they could leave was by the front door. There was at least one attacker with a gun who had a clear line of sight to their motel room. So they would have to distract this attacker somehow and slip past him.

"Right. We're getting out of here. The closest stairs are to the left from the breezeway. Out there, it's a straight shot down to the parking lot. We can cut left at the edge and make it around the front of the building."

"We need to…" Frank trailed off, grimacing in pain.

Micah snatched a chair from the desk and held it above his head. "I know, Frank. Don't worry, I've got this. You open that door, I'm chucking this thing, and then we're off. Okay?"

Frank nodded and rose to his feet. "I can do this."

"I know you can."

Frank yanked back the door and Micah hurled the chair with all his strength. It clanged off the railing and tumbled down one flight to the ground. The metal railing reverberated in both directions, like a tuning fork.

A couple of gunshots followed, and Micah dashed out onto the breezeway, hoping like hell that Frank had the strength to follow him.

He cut left toward the stairs, and he did hear Frank behind him, his heavy footfalls thudding on the concrete breezeway, making it shimmy.

Noises came from below.

Micah reached the stairs and spun to see Frank nearly hyperventilating as he tried to keep pace. His eyes looked glazed over. Despite it all, he pushed through and met Micah at the stairs as the attackers barked orders at each other.

Micah made out two distinct voices. Tried to get a look at the parking lot, but his vision was a blur of motion.

He grabbed Frank's hand and pulled him down the

stairs, hustling around the bend toward the front of the motel. They skirted the fence line to reach the alley.

No gunshots or footfalls coming after them. They hadn't been seen.

Micah and Frank rounded the building as a chorus of new voices arose. Shouts and now screams of motel inhabitants echoed around the building. Micah dragged Frank along the alley, toward the motel office.

"Frank, where's your .357?"

Frank closed his eyes. "Crap. I wasn't thinking. It's back in the room. I'm so sorry."

Micah gritted his teeth as he threw back the office door, and guided Frank into the office. Motel counter on one side, a set of chairs and a continental breakfast bar on the other. Past the chairs were elevators and a hallway.

Micah sat him in a chair, and then Frank groaned while he clenched his side. His eyes rolled back in his head as he tried to get comfortable.

A distraught man behind the office counter was babbling into the telephone. When Micah looked his way, the man slammed his hand against a button on the wall, which caused a gate to slide down from the ceiling.

"I'm talking to the police right now!"

"I'm not the shooter, damn it," Micah said.

"Micah," Frank said, growling. "We have to hurry. We need to get to the car and get the hell out of here. Forget the gun in the room and find out how we can sneak to the car."

"It's okay," Micah said. "You stay here. I'm going to deal with this."

Frank nodded and slumped into the chair, beaten and exhausted. Micah looked around the manager's office for ideas. He didn't have much to work with. An *out of order* sign hung between the two elevators.

The hallway beyond the elevators led to the outside, back to the parking lot they'd come from. There were no inner stairs to reach the second floor. His hand instinctively went to the bump in his pocket where Boba Fett should be, but he found the pocket smooth. Like Frank's gun, Boba was back in the motel room. He felt naked without the little plastic space bounty hunter.

Was it worth going back to get Boba? No, that would be crazy. Still, Micah wanted it. Wanted that comfort of knowing his trinket was with him.

He crept toward the door to the outside, his eyes on the safety glass cutout. Looking for movement outside.

When he was close enough to bring the parking lot into focus, he spotted two heads poking out above the trunk of a small sedan. This was good news. They hadn't figured out that Frank and Micah had escaped around the side of the building. They would soon, though. They might have only stopped to reload their weapons or to make a plan to search the motel.

Either way, they wouldn't sit there forever.

Micah was outnumbered and outgunned. The cops would be here at any second. If these two gunmen died in a shootout or escaped when the sirens approached, Micah would lose any chance of getting information. Who these guys were. If they were connected to the Crossroads casino people, or beautiful backstabber Olivia, or maybe even the cartel.

They might know the identity of the lookalike in the morgue. If Micah had a chance to learn what they knew, he had to take it.

He pressed open the door while the two gunmen remained hidden behind the car. Thirty feet in front of Micah, only the car and a stretch of motel back porch separating them. What were they waiting for?

He considered taking them on directly. But that would be suicide. He had to sneak back up to the room to get Frank's gun. It was the only way he could even the odds.

He crept forward, glancing at the stairs. The bulk of the car kept him hidden, but if he made a break for it, it would be too easy for them to gun him down. He needed a distraction but was all out of chairs to throw.

Gunshots blasted down from above. On the second floor of the motel, from a few rooms down from Micah's. The two gunmen returned fire, stepping out into the open to expose themselves.

Micah jumped forward to get a look. The two gunmen were wearing suits, just like the guards at the casino. White men. No reason to think they were cartel.

Another shot came from above and Micah's eyes flicked up to see a man wearing a bathrobe, his wild hair jutting out at odd angles. He was gripping the breezeway railing with one hand. In his other hand was one of the biggest pistols Micah had ever seen. Magnum .44, maybe, although Micah was too far away to know for sure.

"Goddamn bastards!" the man shouted between blasts. His round belly jiggled with each pull of the hand cannon's trigger.

Didn't take Micah long to figure out what was happening here. Some kind of vigilante currently staying at the motel had heard the commotion and decided to come out shooting.

The vigilante clipped one of the gunmen in the leg, who screamed and dropped to the ground. The other gunman stepped in front of him and squeezed off a shot which hit the vigilante in the neck. Fountain of blood streaming down his wifebeater t-shirt, he bent over the breezeway railing and tumbled down to the parking lot. This amateur had never stood a chance, exposing himself like that.

Micah ducked back behind the front of the car as the standing gunman tried to help his injured colleague. He slung his arm over the guy and started dragging him toward the edge of the parking lot. Streaks of blood on the ground followed them.

Sirens echoed in the distance.

The injured gunman had dropped his pistol, a Glock 17. It gleamed in the sun, a few feet from a parked motorcycle.

Micah scrambled after it as the gunmen lurched toward the fence at the edge of the lot. He snatched up the Glock and kept his footfalls quiet. Didn't matter much, because the screams and shouts of the motel inhabitants made everything a chaotic mess of sound. More people had wandered out of their rooms, cellphones to ears. Micah kept his head down, trying not to show his face to anyone above him.

The attackers slipped around the fence, and Micah hurried to catch up with them. He paused at the edge of the fence when he heard voices. They were talking at a normal level, but with street noise, Micah couldn't make out any of the words. Just a babble of sounds.

After a few seconds, he abandoned trying to listen and raised his new gun. With a deep breath to steel himself, he jumped around the edge of the fence.

Only one gunman was there, sitting, resting against the fence, a pool of blood gathering around his leg. Big blond mustache that curled around his lips like a handlebar.

Micah jerked around, looking for the other gunman. He was nowhere to be found. Just an alley between the fence and a row of stores and restaurants.

Go after the missing assailant, or stay here with this injured one? Micah didn't know what to do. He didn't have time to think it through.

Mustache man looked up at Micah.

"That's my gun," he said through a throaty gurgle. The pool of blood was spreading fast. Mustache man's skin turned from tan to pale to nearly white. His hands were open, his bloody palms pointing at the sky. The fingers of his left hand flickered, jerking. This guy would be dead in a matter of seconds.

"Where's the other one?" Micah said. Mustache man

didn't answer, so Micah lifted his Glock and pointed it at the man's face.

The guy laughed. "I'm already dead, you idiot. There's no point in shooting me."

"Why is this happening?" Micah said, his voice approaching a scream. "Why is there a dead man in a morgue that looks exactly like me? Who was he?"

The dying man squinted up at Micah's face. "Oh, wow, he does look a little bit like you. Wait... are you Micah Reed? Holy shit, is it really you?"

Micah snapped his fingers to get the man's attention. "Who is the dead man? What is his name?"

Mustache man coughed, then his head slipped to the side. It jerked once, then settled. His eyes were blank and frozen.

Dead.

The police sirens came closer. On an impulse, Micah snatched the dead man's wallet from his back pocket, hid the gun in his own waistband, and casually walked away.

# CHAPTER TWENTY-SEVEN

B Y THE TIME Micah had returned to the motel office, there were no cops inside because they were now investigating the dead vigilante. They would probably assume the two gunmen had been there to kill him. Like carriage horses with blinders on to block out anything distracting.

No motel manager, either.

Micah wanted to dash back upstairs, grab Frank's gun, but he didn't want to risk it. Hopefully, he could come back for their things later.

Frank was still in the chair, hunched over and groaning. But he smiled when Micah walked in. A meager, level smile.

"What's the story?" Frank said.

"No story. We're alive, not in handcuffs, and we're leaving before anyone can ask us questions. I'll explain on the way to the hospital."

Micah lifted Frank and aided him out to the parking lot, then helped him ease into the rental car passenger seat. As he'd expected, the cops were outside the dead vigilante's room, preparing to kick in the door. The motel manager stood behind them, hands clasped to his chest. Some nearby neighbors had poked their heads out of motel rooms, watching with rapt interest.

Frank reclined his seat and grimaced as his hands massaged his side. The old man didn't seem healthy at all.

Micah started up the car and backed out of the lot. Gave one last look at the cops to make sure they hadn't been seen. The law was too busy kicking the door down and barging into the second story motel room. "Are you sure that's food poisoning?"

"Nope. I'm not sure of anything. Don't know what else it could be, though."

"Do you think maybe Olivia and her partner did that to you?"

"I don't know why they would. If they wanted to kill me, they could have done it in that motel room. They seemed professional; not like the types to hurt me unless they thought it would gain them something."

The logic was sound. Micah dug the dead gunman's wallet out of his pocket. Flipped it open.

"Paul Browne, with an 'e' on the end. Do you know who that is?"

Frank shook his head. "Doesn't ring a bell." But then his mouth dropped open and he sat up a fraction. "Wait. It was a white guy, right?"

"Yes. There were two of them. One died from a bullet to his leg, and the other got away. Paul's the dead one. Must have severed a main artery or something when that wifebeater guy shot him."

"Light hair?"

"I think so," Micah said.

"I know a guy named Browne with an *e* who was part of that Crossroads gang, a long time ago. He'd be an old man now, but he had twin boys, I know that much."

"That's a good place to start. You don't happen to know this address, do you?"

Frank examined the address on the license. "I do, actually. I can show you exactly how to get there. We take 475 toward Grand Blanc, and it's near there."

"I don't think so, Frank. I can find this place with my phone, so you don't need to tag along. I think the smart thing to do is get you to the hospital."

"That can wait, kid. You have to trust me on this. Let me guide you there, because I have a feeling you're going to need me. If we're walking into an ambush, two sets of eyes are better than one."

Micah patted the steering wheel and gritted his teeth. Frank was in bad shape, and Micah didn't want to delay admitting him to the hospital, but the old man seemed insistent on accompanying him. Micah wished he had Boba Fett here with him, but Boba was back in the motel room. Hopefully, he'd be able to return there and collect their things soon enough.

Obviously, they would need a new motel room.

Micah changed lanes and headed for the highway. His thoughts drifted to the pretty girl in the casino, the one with the big blue eyes and bigger boobs and the tray full of drinks. He wondered if she knew what she'd been getting into when she applied for a job at a casino run by skinheads. Micah had to remind himself that rescuing her wasn't his responsibility. Maybe she even liked working for those messed-up people.

He joined Interstate 475 and drove south until Frank advised him to exit on Hill Road. Pretty town, not anything like the industrial concrete and brick of Flint. This was sparse suburbia. Neighborhoods and strip malls in between vast fields of green.

"There's some Michigan lore I haven't been able to figure out," Micah said.

"Go ahead."

"People that live in the Upper Peninsula are Yoopers, right? I heard that on a TV show."

Frank nodded.

"So do you call people that live in the lower peninsula *Lopers?*"

Frank shook his head. "Trolls. Because they live under the bridge that connects upper and lower. Under it, as far as the map goes."

Micah got it, like a light switching on. "Ahh, that makes sense."

He navigated directly to the address on the license, except it wasn't a house, it was a liquor store at the edge of a neighborhood.

"I don't understand," Frank said.

"Old license. Or maybe it was a fake."

"We can fix this. I think I know where the dad used to live. If we find that, maybe we can go from there."

Micah didn't like the way Frank was grimacing with each labored word, but he decided to humor the old man a bit longer.

They drove around for another half hour, Frank thinking that this next street was the one, then coming up empty, then trying another street, and that one not being it either.

After a dozen of these, Micah said, "I don't know if this is going to work, Frank."

"No, it has to. It's just hard to get my bearings. So much has changed."

Micah let this go on for another fifteen minutes because Frank was so determined to figure out the location of this house, and Micah didn't have the heart to shut him down. Micah took another left into a new neighborhood.

Frank sat up, grunting in pain. "Wait. I know that church."

He pointed at a tall white building with a cross jutting from the top. "This is it. Down this street. Browne lives—or lived—on this block, and he was building a brick house with blue siding and a detached garage for his twins to live in. I remember now."

Micah marveled at Frank's recall. "How do you know all this?"

"Paul Browne's dad got into a fist fight with the inspector over the distance of the garage to the curb. Put the poor guy in the hospital. I was the arresting officer, first of a few times I came out to this part of town. It's coming back. Let's keep going, it has to be here nearby."

Micah turned past the church and crept along at a slow pace through the neighborhood. Big green yards, barking dogs, a mix of old and new houses. None of the houses had fences around the yards, which seemed to be standard in Colorado. Also, few of the neighborhood streets had sidewalks.

"There," Frank said. He was pointing at a brick house with a detached garage, but the siding wasn't what Frank had described. More of a pale green.

"That's not blue siding."

"No, but that could be newly replaced. He did build the house twenty-five years ago, you know."

As Micah got a little closer, he noticed something strange. The front door was wide open. He parked two houses down. Pulled the dead gunman's Glock from his waistband and let its scant weight settle in his hand.

He knew Frank wanted to go in with him, but he couldn't allow it. "Okay, you're staying here."

"Believe me, I'd go if I thought I could. Just be careful, kid."

Micah patted Frank on the shoulder and stepped out of the car. He held the gun low but remained ready to wrap his finger around the trigger at any second. He didn't like carrying guns around anymore, but he had to admit it felt a little familiar in his hand. Like the comfort of meeting up with an old girlfriend. His memories of life in the cartel were often like old lovers, ones who were kind and sweet at first but cruel and domineering later.

Micah climbed onto the front porch and tuned his ear at the open door. Couldn't hear any sounds coming from inside.

He marched carefully, gun out in front. Reminded himself to raise it to eye-level if he was going to shoot. Resist the temptation to pull the trigger too quickly. He didn't know this gun, didn't know how much it would kick and throw off his aim. Probably not much, since it was so compact, but you don't ever know a gun's personality until you've fired it at least once.

After crossing the threshold and stepping inside, he immediately knew why it was quiet. There was a man duct taped to a coffee table, blood leaking from a half a dozen stab wounds in his chest. No one else in the house.

Blond hair, just like the dead gunman back at the motel. Maybe he could have been that man's twin brother, but it was impossible to tell because someone had cut this poor bastard's face like carving a turkey.

# CHAPTER TWENTY-EIGHT

**M**ICAH DROVE FRANK back up to a hospital in Flint so they could keep close to the casino. All of this chaos had some connection to those Crossroads people. That part, though, he hadn't figured out.

A body in the morgue that looked like Micah. The plastic surgeon who'd altered him, murdered by employees of the casino. Olivia kidnapping Frank. Questioning him about Micah's past. People showing up to Micah and Frank's motel room to kill them. How did all the pieces fit?

"Someone really cut Browne's face to pieces?" Frank said.

Micah had been trying not to think about it. "Uh-huh."

"Probably wasn't Crossroads who did that. Not their style."

"Unless," Micah said, "he was on the outs with the gang.

They send him to kill us, then they plan to kill him after. But I don't get why they tortured him."

Frank slipped a handkerchief from his back pocket and coughed into it. "None of this crap makes sense."

The giant beige and glass building of the McLaren hospital come into view. Micah had to slam on his brakes when some woman cut him off turning out of a gas station, then the offender offered a shrug when she met Micah's eye. People in Michigan drove like they were always trying to kill you. Didn't do much to settle Micah's nerves.

"Did I ever tell you about Red Sweater Barry?" Frank said.

"I don't think so."

"I met him in Denver, but he was from Michigan. Heard him speak at an AA meeting, and we bonded over memories of Detroit's heyday. You know, back when that town was worth a crap." Frank grinned, lost in a memory. "He used to say that the difference between an alcoholic and a normal person is that a normie *doesn't* throw the cap in the trash after opening a fresh bottle of whiskey."

Micah emitted a little chuckle. "That's funny."

"Anyway, Barry grew up in Alpena." Frank held up a hand with his fingers together and pointed halfway up his index finger. "On the mitten, it's here. Thunder Bay. So one night, Barry's drunk as a skunk and he drives his car off the pier. Even though the water's shallow, he's still in deep enough to sink, so the water's rushing in, he's freaking out, the whole nine yards. Barely made it out alive."

Frank paused to groan and squeeze his side.

Micah pulled into the McLaren parking lot. "Hang on, Frank, we're almost there."

"I'll get to the point," he said, his teeth clenched. "Sometimes, you think you know where you're going and have every intention of getting there under your own power, but you still end up at the bottom of the lake."

Micah chewed on this story as he helped Frank out of the car and into the emergency room entrance of the hospital. The doors swooshed open in front of them.

After Frank had checked in, Micah helped him to a chair in the waiting room. They sat opposite each other, Frank appearing tired and haggard, and Micah feeling the way Frank looked. None of this had gone the way he'd planned. He had no useful information. Maybe trying to uncover the identity of this lookalike had been a colossal waste of time. Dead end after dead end, finding only more questions anytime he looked for answers.

Maybe he never should have let anyone in this town see his face. But they *had* seen his face, whether or not they knew exactly who he was.

"Do you think—" Frank said, but Micah sat bolt upright, cutting him off.

"Holy shit," Micah said.

"What? You got something?"

"Seen my face. Those kids at the casino. Not kids, I mean, but younger guys who were hanging out outside the mall. Rourke and the other two."

"Hanging out?"

"I think they're casing the mall to try to rob the casino. Anyway, one of them asked me if he knew me. He recognized me. Not me, but the lookalike."

Frank nodded. "It makes sense. Someone around town would have had to know him."

"I've got to get my ass back to the mall and find those guys."

"I'll call you from my room after I'm admitted," Frank said. "Whatever you do, Micah, please think it through before you do something you'll regret."

Micah stood and rested a hand on Frank's shoulder. "Don't worry about me, boss. You focus on getting better and let me take care of this."

# CHAPTER TWENTY-NINE

ROURKE AND HIS two friends Ethan and Carter sat quietly, watching the back door of the Dort Mall. No one had come out of that exit in an hour. In the stillness, Rourke thought he could almost hear the sounds of the casino. But he had to be imagining that noise, because it was underground and hundreds of feet in front of him. Had to be his brain playing tricks on him.

They were hidden behind a dumpster at the edge of the parking lot where it met a line of enormous trees. Crouched on plastic buckets. Rourke held an iPad in his hands, tapping out notes about what they had seen over the last few hours.

> 12:30 pm- Man in blue suit takes out trash.
> Does not look around.
> 2:15 pm- Man in blue suit steps outside to

smoke a joint. Outside for less than ten
minutes, does not leave the door area.

3:10 pm- Man in black suit pushes someone
through the door, punches him, and then
closes the door. The pushed man stumbles
to the front lot.

3:55 pm- Man in blue suit takes out trash,
spends a couple minutes walking the
nearby area. His route doesn't take him
out of eyesight of the door.

There was no pattern. No consistency.

Rourke studied the map of the interior that Carter had
drawn for him, based on an undercover mission inside the
casino earlier that week. Carter had drawn a large
rectangle with most of the gaming tables and slots in rows
at the center of it. Cashier in a cage-like room in one
corner, and several other offices lining the outside area of
the larger room. Seemed the same as Rourke remembered
it as a kid.

Entering through this back door was going to be their
best bet since the front would require passing multiple sets
of guards and gatekeepers. If they could just get in that
door. It seemed a nearly impossible task. But, then it would
only be a straight shot down into the casino, and then a
quick jog back to the cashier. Then stick a gun in his or her
face, fill up the duffel bag, then skedaddle out the
back door.

But they couldn't get in that door when it was locked.

Ethan kicked a stray soda can against the dumpster. "I am bored as shit. Let's go pound some beers. It's still happy hour at Pachyderm for another forty-five minutes."

"Keep it down," Carter said. "We don't know if they have surveillance out here."

"We're not doing anything worth spying on," Ethan said.

Rourke held up a hand. "Guys, knock it off. I don't know how much longer we need to stay out here. Something worthwhile might happen. Or, if you two want to go on, I'll hang out and hook up with you at the pub later."

"Why stay?" Ethan said. "What's the point?"

"There's got to be a pattern."

"We've been at this for days," Carter said. "If there was a distinguishable pattern, we would have found it by now."

"Let's just bust in the front. Guns blazing," Ethan said. "Take them all out quickly, then we have the place to ourselves."

"A full-on assault would be suicide," Rourke said.

Ethan grunted. "Not the way I'd do it. They would never see me coming."

"And give people in the mall a chance to look at our faces so they can identify us to the cops?" Rourke said. "Or are you going to kill them too?"

Carter laughed. "People in that ghost town mall? That's funny. Either way, Rourke, we're running out of time to figure out a way into the back door."

Rourke could feel his temperature rising. Yes, they were running out of time, but making everything into a debate wasn't helping. "There are actual people that work at the hockey store. If we walk in there all casual, then go downstairs and start shooting, they'll have seen us. If we walk in there with pantyhose covering our faces or masks or hoodies, they'll warn the mob downstairs. And we're not going to kill the employees for the crime of working at the hockey store. No, going in the front is not an option."

"Then how the hell do we open that back door on command, eh?" Carter said.

Rourke sighed. "I don't know. Crowbar, maybe, if it comes to that. Even though they'll probably hear us doing it and spoil our surprise."

A twig snapped.

"Spoil your surprise of what?" said a voice to their left, one thick with an Irish accent.

All three of them spun around to find a man with a shaved head twenty paces away, leaning out from behind a tree. Shotgun cradled in his hands.

"Get lost," Ethan said. "Who the hell do you think you are, listening to our conversation like that?"

The man shook his head in disgust. "Oh, come on, now. That's just rude."

Ethan reached toward his back pocket and the man cocked his shotgun to stop him.

"Ethan, don't," Rourke said. They'd left the assault rifles back in the car. Pistols weren't a good match for a shotgun. This guy could blast all three of them with one pull of that trigger before Ethan had his weapon out and pointed.

"Yes, Ethan, how about you don't?" said the Irish man.

He inched out from behind the tree, keeping his legs spread far apart as he walked. Maintained the shotgun at Carter, who was standing in the middle of the three of them.

Carter stood quite still, seemingly untroubled. Ethan just looked mad. Rourke didn't understand how his two friends dealt with this kind of pressure. He did not enjoy having a gun pointed at him.

Rourke wore a hunting knife strapped to a sheath on his belt, but he couldn't remember if the safety strap that held it in place was buttoned or unbuttoned. Having to unbutton it would add too much time. The man's finger was wrapped around that shotgun trigger.

Ready to fire.

Irish Man kept advancing. "Exactly what are the three of you doing back here staring at the mall? This wouldn't have anything to do with the casino in the basement would it? Planning on getting a payday, are we? You think you're the first to engineer a shakedown?"

Carter pursed his lips. "We're not into candy bars."

Irish smirked. "Payday. Oh, that sure is clever."

Ethan balled his fists.

Rourke knew that at any second, Ethan was going to try to rush this guy and steal his shotgun from him. And Ethan wouldn't move five feet without having a hole punched in his stomach. Then there'd be no reason for the Irish guy not to blast Rourke and Carter, too.

And Rourke couldn't help but feel responsible for his two friends. This casino job had been his idea. He'd encouraged his friends to join him. He'd been the one to fill his friends' heads with promises of making so much money they wouldn't have to work for years.

He couldn't worry about that now.

"It's none of your business why we're out here," Rourke said.

The Irish man, toothy grin on his face, pivoted the barrel toward Rourke. "Oh, but it is. I work in that establishment. And keeping ruffians like you in check is part of my job."

"Ruffians?" Carter said. "Who are you, Charles Dickens?"

Irish man laughed.

Ethan growled and took a step forward. This caused the Irish man to pivot back toward him, a little too quickly, and he wobbled, off balance. The shotgun barrel tilted up.

Rourke had only a second before the man would right himself. He snatched at his hunting knife. The safety strap was on, but he yanked on the hilt to pull it free.

He whipped the knife forward, and it sailed ten feet, then pierced the man's side. Just the tip of the blade had sunk into his gut, but he still howled and fell backward. The shotgun tumbled into the grass near his head.

He tried to grab at the shotgun.

Rourke and Ethan were on him in a flash. Rourke snatched the shotgun away from him as Ethan drew his pistol and pointed it at Irish Man's face.

"Ethan, no!" Carter said. "No guns. They'll hear it."

"He's right," Rourke said as he pulled the knife from the Irish man, which caused him to shudder and moan.

"You little shit punks," Irish Man said. "Harvey is going to cut off your balls and feed them to his dog when he finds out about this. You want to mess with Crossroads? Do you have any idea who you're trying to rob?"

Rourke wasn't sure if he knew the answer to that question anymore. But they'd attacked someone who worked there. They were committed to going all the way.

And he was also committed to dealing with this current situation. This man on the grass, he had to be eliminated or everything they'd worked for would fracture into pieces.

Rourke dragged the blade across the Irish man's neck to silence him. Rourke couldn't believe how easy it was; just a little pressure and then a swipe of his hand, and the sharpened blade did the rest of the work.

A trail of red followed the knife, his neck splitting open to reveal the inside of his throat. He squirmed and flailed, his hands trying to stem the tide of blood rushing down over the collar of his shirt.

But it was pointless. Rourke had cut him deep. There was no amount of pressure that could close the wound. The Irish man stopped working his mouth open and closed as his breathing halted. He spasmed a couple times, then went motionless. The only sound coming from him was the faint seeping of blood coming from the gash in his neck.

Rourke didn't stop to think about how it was the first

person he'd ever killed. In his head, he'd rehearsed the casino break-in scenario so many times, he felt as if he'd already killed those skinhead assholes a dozen times over.

But this was real. He'd ended a life.

"Holy shit," Carter said. "He's dead."

"Yeah, he is," Ethan said, then he spit on him. "Nazi shitbag."

"There's going to be a lot more of this when we get inside that casino," Rourke said. "Are you guys okay with that?"

Ethan nodded, no fear or hesitancy in his expression.

Rourke faced Carter, who was still standing behind them. Raised his eyebrows.

"Yeah, yeah, I'm okay with this," Carter said. "We had to do it. He would have killed us. I have an miniscule amount of sympathy for these racist pieces of garbage."

Rourke had no sympathy either, but he was beginning to understand the weight of these actions. How deeply involved they were now.

He stood, and a bolt of panic gripped Rourke's chest. Parked forty feet away from the dumpster was a small sedan. And a man stood next to it, car door open, just staring.

Rourke squinted. "You."

The man raised his hand in a meek wave. "Hi, guys."

# CHAPTER THIRTY

ICAH PARKED HIS car behind the mall just as Rourke whipped the knife at the bald man's gut. Rourke had some skill with the knife, but luck appeared to guide his hand. The odds of a perfect throw like that had to have been slim.

Micah watched as they wrestled the shotgun away from him and then slashed his neck open. In one quick motion, Rourke ended this man's life. The man on the ground kicked a couple times, but he had a quick and clean death.

While it had been a brutal and decisive move, they still appeared hesitant, both before and after. Micah could see the conflict written in the eyes of the one who had used the knife. Rourke.

This had been an impulsive and unexpected development. The dead man had probably surprised them. Maybe they were inexperienced enough not to account for patrols in the woods behind the mall. This shotgun-wielding man was probably a casino guard out on watch, had caught them on the property, and hadn't anticipated these kids being armed or being willing to defend themselves.

After they'd killed the guard, they all stared at the body for a few seconds, mute and wide-eyed. These guys had never done this kind of thing before. That much was plain. This fact made them dangerous, because now they had skin in the game and a lack of knowledge about how to handle themselves.

Regret would lead to carelessness. Micah knew all about that.

He got out of the car and kept a hand on the pistol in his waistband. He'd thought these three would-be casino robbers to be harmless, but they obviously weren't. Needed to make sure he didn't startle them, so he shut the car door carefully.

Rourke turned to ask his longhaired friend something, and his eyes jumped wide open when he saw Micah.

Micah waved.

"You were here yesterday," Rourke said.

"That's right. Isn't it funny how so much seems to revolve around this broken-down shopping mall behind me? This crazy building full of a lifetime of carnie junk?"

"I don't think it's funny at all," the longhaired one said.

Micah ignored this and nodded at the one he assumed was the leader. "You're Rourke, but I didn't catch your friends' names."

The heavy one lifted the shotgun and pointed it at Micah. This one knew better than to put his finger on the trigger, at least. "My name is none of your goddamn business."

"You must have to use tiny print on your business cards, then. That's got to be a pain in the ass." Micah took the hand off his pistol and relaxed. Despite the dead man in the grass, the shotgun wielding big guy, and Rourke holding a bloody knife, Micah didn't get the sense that he was in danger.

They all looked scared shitless. Aware that they were now in deep and not sure what to do about it.

"What do you want?" Rourke said.

Micah took a step forward and the big guy eyed him. He recalled this one's name from the other day. Ethan.

Ethan cocked the shotgun and snarled. Now he did wrap his finger around the trigger, and Micah had no reason to think he wouldn't shoot. Ethan was clearly the brazen one of the group.

Micah halted. Maybe they were scared shitless enough to keep acting on impulse. Maybe they thought Micah was another employee of the casino, and they would have every right to shoot him.

Perhaps he was in danger, after all.

"Look," Micah said. "I tried to tell you guys yesterday that I don't care what you're into. I can only assume you're casing the casino here to do a break-in. And this poor dead guy on the ground caught you, just like I did. The thing is, I don't give two shits what you guys want with this place. I don't work for the casino people. I'm not here for anything related to that."

"Then I'll ask you again," Rourke said, "what do you want?"

"When I saw you before, you asked me if you knew me." Micah pointed at the longhaired one. "You did."

"So?" the longhair said.

"Who do you think I look like?"

Rourke and his two companions exchanged a few uneasy glances, all of them reluctant to speak. Seconds dripped by in silence. Ethan maintained his dagger eyes with Micah, but Rourke appeared to be considering the question, at least.

"If we tell you who you remind us of," Rourke said, "what's it worth to you?"

Micah mulled it over. They had to believe he had some kind of angle in all this, and they had no good reason to trust him. He could offer to keep quiet about the dead body on the ground, but then they might realize that they'd be better off shooting him to keep him quiet. They hadn't looked like the type of crew to do that, but Micah now realized he might be putting too much faith in his own intuition. That hadn't often worked out so well in the past.

His best bet would be to come clean about what he wanted, but he also had to offer them something in return. Something he could do for them that they hadn't been able to do themselves.

Micah tilted his head back at the mall, and they were in a clear line of sight to the back door that led down into the casino.

"Have you guys been out here for a while, watching that back door?"

Rourke nodded.

"Trying to figure out a way to get in?"

Rourke nodded again.

"Do any of you know how to pick a lock?"

Ethan said nothing, and the longhair averted his eyes. Rourke shook his head.

"Then today's your lucky day," Micah said. "I can teach you exactly how to pick the lock to that back door."

# CHAPTER THIRTY-ONE

**P**ARKED NEAR THE back of the mall, watching from the side view mirror, Olivia saw the whole thing. Those three young men getting caught snooping, then killing their assailant, and then Micah rolling up on them. Then, him showing the three of them something near the back door. She couldn't tell what he'd shown them, but it was a game-changer. The three men had gone from pointing guns at him to shaking his hand before Micah went on his way.

Micah certainly was a charmer. On the doomed flight from Fresno, twisting into certain death, she'd almost felt safe in his embrace. Even with everything she knew about his past, she hadn't considered his danger in the moment. That was the power of Micah Reed's persuasiveness.

Even though sitting next to him on that airplane and the flirting had been by design, the WitSec ex-criminal formerly known as Michael McBriar had a certain amount of appeal to him. A kind of socially awkward little boy cuteness. Mixed with that bad-boy dangerousness and manipulation, that made for a red-flag-topped cocktail.

Jeremy leaned over her and adjusted her mirror so he could see. "What do you think that was about?"

"No idea. An exchange of services, I would guess. Had to be something significant, for them not to kill Micah after seeing what they did to that guy on patrol."

"Should we follow Micah? I don't like that he's back here at the casino."

Olivia chewed on it. She did want to follow him and see where he was going, but that wasn't what they were supposed to be doing. All their efforts were supposed to shift away from Micah Reed and move toward the Crossroads gang.

But, she had to admit that she felt a small rush of excitement seeing Micah again, even though he had shaved his head, which was not a good look for him. And those thick glasses changed his face quite a bit. He was trying to disguise himself, obviously.

Something about him had stuck with her, and she didn't like that. Made her feel not in control.

"No," she said. "We don't need anything from him. He didn't kill Logan King, so we're done with him."

Olivia knew they should probably kill him. Get him out of the way. But, for some reason, she resisted what she knew to be the right course.

"It's good to have a name to finally put to the John Doe,"

Jeremy said. "Even though it was difficult to extract the information."

She pivoted in her chair. "You're the one who carved up that gangster in Grand Blanc. You didn't have to do that."

"Well, we knew Micah was on his way. There wasn't much time."

Olivia patted his hand and offered a reassuring smile. "I know. I'm not angry with you. We do need to be careful about the footprint we leave, though. This isn't Kabul."

"Understood."

He moved his hand so his index finger was on top of hers. He stroked her finger and gave her *that look*. Her instinct told her to pull her hand back and say *not now*, but it felt good. She wanted more.

"Maybe we stop by the hotel after this?" he said.

"That sounds like a good idea." She cleared her throat. Needed to focus. She turned back to the side view mirror and adjusted it again so she could watch the three unknown men get back into their car. "Did you ever figure out what was on Micah's thumb drives? What those spreadsheets were?"

Jeremy put his hands back into his lap, not pouting this time. The anticipation of getting laid would be enough to ensure his happiness, for now. "Nothing definitive about the spreadsheets. Best I can figure, it's stolen cartel data. From their books, maybe, to use as leverage. I don't know."

Stolen, probably like that business card with the image of the wolf. No way a mid-level thug in Luis Velasquez's drug army would earn an El Lobo calling card like that.

Unless he'd been more important than she'd been led to believe. Some of his files were above her security clearance, after all.

"Good enough," she said. "Maybe we can use that data to our advantage."

"How?"

She shrugged. "No idea, but we'll keep it in our back pockets for now. I think our next step is finding out who these three yokels are, and making sure they don't mess everything up. With all of this cloak and dagger stuff they have going on, I have a feeling they're trying to rob the casino."

"They could make all of it blow up in our faces," Jeremy said. "Burst in at the wrong time and alert everyone."

Olivia played with a chunk of her hair, checking it for split ends. "Maybe. Or maybe they're exactly what we need."

## CHAPTER THIRTY-TWO

**M**ICAH DROVE ALONG the streets of Flint with one name dancing on his mind. Logan King. That was the identity of the John Doe who had been surgically altered to look like him. The name at the heart of this whole mess, the mutilated corpse that had set everything in motion.

Logan King. A dead man with Micah's face.

The three break-in guys from the mall had known him in high school but hadn't seen him around for years. He'd been a couple years older, and not in the same social circle as Rourke, Carter, and Ethan. Rowdy guy, apparently in and out of trouble for most of his life. Quite a bit like Micah had been until his life flipped upside down after the cartel.

But the casino break-in kids still knew Logan's mother's address, and Micah was on his way there now. There had to be answers in that house. Had to be something that could make sense of all this mess.

A buzzing came from his pocket and Micah snatched his phone. Unknown number.

"Hello?"

"Hey, kid."

"Frank? How are you? Did they give you something for the food poisoning?"

Frank moaned. "It's not food poisoning. Appendicitis. Hard to believe an old man like me never had his appendix out, right?"

"Ahh, that makes more sense, because I've never seen food poisoning like you had."

"Mystery solved."

"Well, at least, they know what it is. Now you can get better."

"After these quacks cut me open, sure," Frank said. "But it also means I'm out of commission for a couple days, so whatever happens with John Doe, you're on your own."

A bolt of excited energy pulsed in Micah's chest. "Speaking of that, I made progress. I know who he is. I got the name, and I'm on my way to his mom's house now."

Frank hesitated. "Be careful, kid. If this young man died so someone could collect the bounty on your head, maybe you don't jump right into the middle of it. Maybe it's best to leave it alone."

"But we've come so far, Frank. This is the home stretch."

"I worry about you getting in too deep. There's nothing

you could do personally that you can't accomplish by making an anonymous call to the cops."

Micah peered over at the Glock in the passenger seat, stolen from the gangster who'd bled out near the motel. Having the gun was supposed to give him confidence, but it didn't. Micah had mostly been running on curiosity and adrenaline. That wouldn't last. "Don't worry about me."

Frank paused again, and Micah knew exactly what Frank was thinking. That he would worry no matter what.

"When I'm done there, I'm going to swing by the motel and get our stuff. I'll check in somewhere else, somewhere no one knows about. I can do this cleanly."

"I know you can," Frank said. "Just be careful."

Micah made some assurances and they ended the call. And even though Micah had done dangerous things before without Frank by his side, this was one time he wished he could have had the old man's help. Micah was in over his head, no doubt about that. And Frank had a lifetime of experience with this sort of thing.

And then Micah felt selfish for wanting Frank at his side because his mentor was sick. Frank was entitled to take care of himself, wasn't he?

Micah drove into the nearby town of Burton. He was constantly surprised by how lush everything was, as soon as he left the immediate Flint area. Such towering trees and endless fields of green. He'd always pictured Michigan as a northern industrial place, full of machinery and smog and dirty snow. But expectation and truth were often far apart. He should have had enough life lessons by now to know better.

But this suburb still had its share of liquor and gun stores. A mix of sad people standing on street corners and shiny new cars traversing the streets.

Micah checked the address of the King residence, scrawled on the back of a napkin from Big John Steak and Onion. He navigated to Belsay Road and stopped in front of 3152. Like all the other houses around, this one was set a little back from the road, with no fence and no sidewalk. Sign out front read *dog contained by invisible fence*. Micah hoped he wasn't about to run into a Rottweiler or something meaner.

He parked in the driveway behind a Chevy Malibu. Brand new, still had the temporary dealer license on it. He slipped the gun into his waistband and practiced reaching for it. No reason to think Logan King's mother would attack him, but he'd had enough surprises on this trip to know better than to assume.

This city seemed hell bent on killing him.

With one last deep breath for encouragement, he walked to the front door and rang the doorbell. Music and the sound of running water drifted through an open window near the front door.

He rang the bell again and the running water ceased. The front door opened, and there stood a woman, drying her hands on a dish towel. Late forties or early fifties.

Her mouth dropped open. She tried to speak but nothing coherent came out. He had abandoned the fake glasses and removed the contacts beforehand, to remove any doubt.

A little dog rushed across the room and sniffed at Micah's feet.

"You know who I am, don't you?" he said.

"You look just like him."

"Logan King. That's who I look like, right? Can I come in and talk to you about it?"

Tears welled at the corners of her eyes. The dog fled into the living room and leaped onto the couch. Gave a single, high-pitched bark.

The woman licked her lips. "You shouldn't be here. I don't know how you found me, but I wish you wouldn't have. It's not safe for you to be here."

"Then why don't you let me in before someone sees me?"

She paused, but only for a moment, and then stepped aside to admit Micah into the house. The dog growled.

The woman waved him toward a lime green couch opposite a massive television. Heavy carpet underfoot. He sat next to the dog, and the little beast resumed sniffing at the leg of his jeans. "Would you like a drink? I have beer, wine, or I can mix you something."

"I don't drink," Micah said.

The woman smiled a sad smile at him and had a seat on the floor, next to the TV. She crossed her legs and rested her hands on her knees, in a meditative kind of pose. "Then you're not much like my Logan beyond looks. He liked to drink. A lot."

Micah almost smiled, because he and Logan were more alike than this woman realized. Before sobriety, not a day went by that Micah didn't try to escape into a bottle. He sometimes forgot he was only seven months removed from that life.

"It's what killed him, you know," she said.

Micah leaned forward, which made the dog growl. "What do you mean, it killed him?"

She pointed at her stomach. "His liver was failing. Hard to believe, I know. Twenty-seven years old and his liver was giving out on him already. And even knowing that, he still wouldn't give up the drinking."

"Alcoholism is an insidious disease."

She nodded at this. "I've watched it happen to so many in my family, it feels normal. How does something so terrible become normal? When you start going to more funerals than weddings and no one thinks that's strange?"

He didn't have an answer for her, so he kept quiet.

She swept a chunk of hair out of her eyes. "I'm Yvette."

"Micah Reed, but you already knew that."

She sighed. "Not really. If you came here looking for answers, Mr. Reed, I'm afraid I don't have any for you. Logan did what he did for me. It was his final act, and the only unselfish act he'd ever done."

Micah leaned closer as the pieces fell into place. Logan had given himself up willingly to have plastic surgery, and then he'd let them kill him. But Micah still didn't know why. Would Crossroads go to so much trouble over a bounty?

"What does Crossroads really want? What aren't you telling me?"

Yvette's neck tensed. She was starting to close up. "I never should have said anything. Never should have let you in here. If you want to know the truth, you're going to have to talk to Harvey down at the casino. But if you intend to do that, you need to hurry. They're packing up everything and leaving the day after tomorrow."

# PART III

RED SWEATER BARRY

# CHAPTER THIRTY-THREE

**R**OURKE SCOOTED THE seat closer to his workbench and ran a shaky hand over the wooden stock of his AK-47. It was scuffed and worn, the wood streaked with tiny imperfections.

The only sound in his garage was the ticking of a wall clock. His sister had gone out for the evening, so he'd earned a couple hours to himself. Time to think, or better yet, not think.

He'd killed a man. Dragged a knife across his throat and ended his life. The man had been trying to kill Rourke and his two friends, but that didn't give Rourke the comfort he might have expected with justified self-defense killing. That man had a mother and father, maybe even a wife and kids. Someone would miss him. Someone would mourn him.

The way the knife cut into the Irish man, slicing flesh open like raw chicken. The way his eyes jumped wide as the blood leaked out of his neck and onto the grass. The way he tried to speak but only blood dribbled out of his moving lips. Tried to stop his life from flooding out of his open neck.

Maybe it was the fact that Rourke knew he'd have to do more killing before it was all over. More killing before the Crossroads gang was eradicated and he could recover all the money his father had wasted at those card tables. Make the past right and get rich while doing it.

It sounded so good, in theory; killing bad people. Now that he'd started putting it into practice, it didn't seem so much like checking off items from a list anymore.

He wanted it to be easy. To take pleasure in ruining these casino assholes. But instead, this made him question everything in his life up to this point. What would Rourke's obituary read after he died trying to rob this casino?

The garage door rattled, and Rourke snatched the dirty towel on his workbench to cover up the rifle. He crossed the garage and peered out the window to see Carter standing there, his arms crossed. Impatient.

"Open up," Carter said through the door.

Rourke thumbed the button to raise the garage door, and Carter slipped his hands into his pocket, now seeming relaxed.

"Sup, dude?" Carter said, grinning.

Rourke raised his palms. "Not much."

Carter entered the garage, smacking Rourke on the shoulder as he passed him. He took a seat on the hood of

Rourke's car. "Two more days. You getting excited? I don't even know if I'll be able to sleep tonight."

"Excited isn't the word I'd use," Rourke said as he jabbed the button again to lower the garage door.

"What's with the dour face? We have two days to plan and get this shit ready. Only two more days until we make a name for ourselves. Show these racist jerkwads what happens when they think they can run Flint."

Rourke wanted to match Carter's enthusiasm. Rourke was the one who should have had the motivation. The personal vendetta. There seemed to be no trouble getting Carter excited, and Ethan was always hungry for a fight. Maybe the three of them didn't have a unified goal with this robbery, but the three goals put together should have given Rourke the boost he needed.

"Are you going to tell me what's wrong with you?" Carter said.

Rourke considered a few different ways to talk about it. Couldn't find phrasing he liked, so he spit it out. "That guy we killed. I keep seeing his face."

Carter took a few breaths and scooted up the hood of the car so his feet dangled off the edge. "That was messed up. But it had to happen."

"You seem so calm about it."

Carter ran a finger along the car's hood. "Sure, I look that way. It's easy to compare your insides to other people's outsides and come up short. But when you get right down to it, it was him or us, and I don't feel bad about what we did. Who knows how many people that guy had killed before."

"Good point. I hadn't thought about it like that."

"Why do you think you keep seeing his face?"

Rourke turned his head away as he realized he didn't want to discuss it anymore. Hashing it out like a therapy session wasn't going to undo what they'd done.

So, he changed the subject and moved on to logistical problems. "I think we should get more info. We need to learn something concrete about what we're going to find in there on Saturday night. Where the money is, how much we can expect to clear, and when it'll be the least-guarded."

Carter pushed his glasses up his nose. "Okay, that sounds like the start of a plan. What did you have in mind?"

"Maybe we snatch one of them."

"I like where your head's at. How do we do that?"

Rourke opened the mini-fridge and removed two cans of beer. Tossed one to Carter. "We don't know their exact schedule, but we know they use that back door to take out the garbage a few times a day, at least. I say tomorrow, we wait right outside that back door and get one of them. Pop him in the trunk and take him somewhere."

"You don't sound convinced that this is a good idea."

Rourke hadn't realized his voice had wavered. "Am I crazy to be freaked out by all this? We're going in there armed with assault weapons. We could die."

"Dude, this was your idea. I'm totally on board with it,

but if you're feeling any trepidation, maybe we should call it off."

Rourke debated this idea. Would he feel like a total failure if they decided to abandon the casino raid? They'd already come so far, had made so much progress and invested so much time. After blowing all of his money on the AKs, he had nothing left.

"Or," Carter said as he sipped his beer, "you could just stop being a pussy about it."

Rourke chuckled. "It's that black and white, eh?"

"Of course not. Yes, it's dangerous. We might get shot at. But think of what we stand to gain. We'll be swimming in so much money, we could buy the damn Dort Mall, if we wanted. We could shut that bitch down and have our own private soirées there. Think about it: our own personal shopping mall."

"I got my first ever handjob behind that mall, when I was fourteen. Tiffany Catanzaro."

"Exactly," Carter said. "Dort should be on the goddamn historic register."

"Never thought I'd be a shopping mall owner. I kinda like that."

Carter finished his beer, crossed the room, and put a hand on Rourke's shoulder. "You'll be a motherfucking entrepreneur. You can put up a plaque outside the mall commemorating Tiffany Catanzaro stroking your cock for the first time. People will put flowers underneath it. And all we have to do is snatch one of these bastards, find out what we need to know, and then we get rich."

CHAPTER THIRTY-FOUR

WHEN HE COULD see that questioning Yvette was a waste of time, Micah gave up. She kept answering every question with "talk to Harvey," and wouldn't offer him anything else. He didn't know if he was done with her, but he didn't see any point in interrogating her further that night. Didn't want to harass a woman who'd lost her son only a week before.

Maybe she needed time to reflect and let his involvement sink in. She could come to terms with the fact that she could still do some good here, if she made that choice.

He drove back to Flint, stopped by the old motel, and parked on the far side of the street. Watched. He checked every angle to make sure no one noticed him or had eyes on the motel room.

When he was satisfied, he gathered his and Frank's belongings from the room and left. Didn't bother to check out, because the motel office might have wanted to know why they'd abandoned their room in the middle of a gunfight and therefore weren't around to talk to the cops.

Yellow police tape marked a room on the second floor. The vigilante's room, the one who had shot one of the attackers in the leg, then tumbled to his death in the motel parking lot. Whatever that guy had been seeking, hopefully, he'd found it in a glorious action hero death.

Micah finally had Boba Fett's severed plastic head back in his pocket, which made him feel a little closer to normal. He left and drove around for a half hour to find a new motel, making sure that he wasn't being followed. He committed lots of extra left turns and drove down neighborhood streets to locate any possible tails. He just had to hope this Crossroads gang wasn't sophisticated enough to have satellite tracking.

Olivia would have it, that was for sure. If she were working for the government as a contractor, she'd probably have access to all kinds of high-tech equipment. She could have Micah picked up at any time by the cops, for any reason.

But she'd told Frank they weren't interested in him. Maybe Micah believed that, and maybe not. It didn't matter. If she wanted to speak with him and explain herself, he might listen. Or he might tell her to go to hell.

Either way, he couldn't waste any energy worrying about her right now.

He found a motel not far from Interstate 475 and checked in. Seedy place, a room that smelled of decaying soup, but it was nestled in a more secluded location than the motel they'd been discovered at before. There was a door that led into the adjoining room. Might prove useful.

He set Boba Fett on the nightstand. Felt safe here, for now. The room had double beds, and as he stared at the perfectly tucked bedspread, he thought of Frank. Hoped he was getting the care he needed at the hospital.

Micah walked out of the motel room to check the entrances and exits. He needed a better escape plan if someone else came to call, unlike they'd had at the first motel. That poor planning had almost gotten the both of them killed.

He leaned over the railing, breathing in the tepid night air. Quiet in this part of town.

A sleek black car pulled into the lot, and Micah's jaw dropped open when he saw the passenger. Olivia. The driver, he didn't recognize, but Micah made eye contact with Olivia and held it until the car parked across the lot, a couple hundred feet away.

He hadn't seen her since the Denver airport. Since getting her phone number a few minutes after they'd had a near-death experience together. He carried that number on a slip of paper in his pocket, and now wondered if it was fake. He hadn't called it yet.

She sat in the car, holding his eye contact. Didn't make any move to leave her seat. He felt an urge to bound down the stairs, rush across the lot, accuse her of all manner of things. But why? What would that accomplish?

She wasn't the person she'd said she was. He had to accept that and move on, whatever that meant. Yet another nugget of proof that Micah's new post-WitSec life was meant to be solitary.

He shook his head, disgusted. Didn't want to talk to her. As he turned to leave, he caught a flash of disappointment on her face. Didn't care.

Micah went inside, locked the door, and slid onto the bed to consider his options. Logan's mom Yvette hadn't told him everything. That much was for sure. Harvey and his Crossroads casino gang had killed Logan, and the logical theory was that they'd done it to collect the bounty on Micah's head. But the pieces didn't all fit together. Micah didn't know how much the bounty was, but it couldn't be enough to inspire Crossroads to do all this work.

Something else was happening here, but what?

He couldn't find a logical path to answer that question. And the longer he ran in that circle of thought, the more time he was wasting. Yvette had said Crossroads was abandoning the casino, but not why.

Micah wondered if Rourke and his crew knew about that. If they did know, they'd probably bump any possible timeframe, to rob the casino on its last operational night. To take advantage by shooting up the place while it was in a transition.

And if they did that, they might spoil Micah's chance of finally learning the truth.

That couldn't happen.

He had to get into that casino before they did and confront Harvey. Put a gun to the Nazi bastard's head and make him tell the truth. Get justice for this Logan kid.

But why? Micah didn't even know anymore.

*Selfless act.*

He now realized he'd given up on Yvette too quickly. She had secrets.

He could barely keep his eyes open any longer, he was so tired. But the next step of the plan would involve a return to the King house in the morning. Yvette hadn't wanted to talk to him, but he could get answers some other way.

# CHAPTER THIRTY-FIVE

**O**LIVIA AND JEREMY crouched behind the dumpster, in the exact same spot the crew of three amateur casino robbers had sat, watching the back of the mall. Except now, Olivia was watching the three of *them*, positioned on either side of the back door. A little bit of research had revealed their names to be Rourke Patterson, Carter DeLeo, and Ethan Greenberg. Local amateur criminals with notions of taking their enterprise to the next level.

Olivia had seen this scenario played out dozens of times. It never worked out for the small-time crooks. Instead of becoming big-time, they usually ended up dead.

Rourke's father had a gambling problem, which explained the choice for their current operation. Revenge/robbery, most likely.

"I thought you might stop by my room last night,"

Jeremy said. In the pre-dawn light, she could barely make out his features.

"I was tired."

"It's just… the way you were at dinner… playing with my knee under the table."

She yawned. It was too early to deal with this. "It feels good to flirt, Jeremy. Sometimes I want more. Sometimes I don't."

"But do you see how I could construe that to be a mixed signal?"

She kept thinking about seeing Micah outside his motel room, how he'd worn that look of disdain on his face. She didn't know why, but his scowl unsettled her. "What do you want? You want to be my boyfriend? Is that it? Most guys would be perfectly fine with an occasional no-strings fling."

He crossed his arms. Now he was sulking. "Maybe I'm not most guys."

"Well, you know what? I'm married, so that's all there is to it."

He scowled, which happened whenever Olivia brought up her husband. She didn't like to do that, but Jeremy's whiny desperation had left her no choice.

"Can we please focus on our task at hand?" she said.

"Fine. Think they're hoping to snatch someone and get information?"

"I think that's exactly what they're trying to do. They were making notes on the comings and goings of mall employees yesterday, and now they suspect someone's about to walk out of that door."

"What could they hope to find out? How much money is inside or something like that?"

Olivia tugged at her right eyebrow, twisting the edge of it between her thumb and forefinger. "No idea. These little robbers are quite a mystery."

"But you have some kind of plan to use them to our advantage."

"Maybe," she said. "Our main directive is still making sure Crossroads doesn't get spooked before they abandon ship. Exposing them so we can apprehend the key figures."

Jeremy pivoted toward her. "Apprehending them? You never said anything about that before. We were only supposed to pull strings, keep activity restricted to the private sector so the feds wouldn't have to show their faces. Not get directly involved."

"The parameters changed. I got word from the boss last night."

He sighed. "This is why I hate government contracts. Always changing their damn minds. So if we need to ensure this event happens, we're going to have to eliminate these three."

"Maybe."

The back door opened and out stepped a man in a black suit, unlit cigarette dangling from his lips. Longhaired Carter snatched the man's arm to unbalance him, and big Jewish-looking Ethan smacked the man over the head with something cylindrical.

The man tumbled to the ground, and the three casino robbers snatched him up, tossed him into the trunk of their car, and jumped in after him. Lightning-quick. After the car had disappeared around the corner and to the front of the mall, the back parking lot returned to its desolate silence.

"What now?" Jeremy said.

"Now we see what they're going to do with him. We'll kill them if we have to, but first, we find out where they're going."

## CHAPTER THIRTY-SIX

MICAH STOOD IN front of Yvette King's door as the sun rose above the trees to the east. Not quite the same spectacular purple and orange colors of a Colorado sunrise, but the sky did burn a nice shade of pink before slipping into a flat blue.

In Micah's dream last night, pieces of the plane had splintered away, but the frame of the airplane kept flying. As sections of the walls broke and sank to the ground, the seats and the passengers in them kept careening through the air, oblivious to the chaos around them. No screams of panic. Just a few hundred airplane seats, floating in space. Only Micah was aware of the danger they were all facing.

And he knew also he was asleep, but that hadn't stopped him from feeling his pulse race. Hadn't stopped him from wanting to dream-puke.

He couldn't turn off his feelings.

Olivia and her male companion had been gone when

he'd left the motel that morning. Whatever they wanted, they hadn't bothered him.

Now, standing in front of Yvette's door, the insanity of all Micah's plans weighed on him. He didn't have a good grasp on what he hoped to accomplish here, at her house this morning. He just knew he needed *something* from her. And wouldn't leave until he got it.

She opened the door before he had a chance to knock. Wearing a bathrobe, spatula in her hand. The sharp smell of bacon wafted from the kitchen.

She shook her head as her little dog tried to jump on him. The dog made it as far as his knee, then retreated from the room when Micah shook his leg.

"You shouldn't have come back," she said. "I can't help you."

Micah didn't ask to be invited in. He stepped forward and Yvette didn't stop him. He had no desire to hurt her or even threaten her, but in order for Micah to obtain the info he desired, he had to seem like someone who'd demand answers.

Yvette shut the door behind him and clutched her spatula to her chest. "I don't know what else I can tell you. I let go of Logan a long time ago."

Micah spun and put his hands on his hips. "You said the Crossroads gang was abandoning the casino. I need to know why."

She frowned. "What good will it do?"

"Do you know what they did to him? What they did to

your son? How they burned him, cut him, turned his body into discarded meat?"

She put a hand to her mouth and stumbled back a step. "They did what?"

Micah hadn't thought it through. He assumed she'd already known this, maybe she'd been to see the body, but her reaction meant she was oblivious. He wished he'd never said anything, but he couldn't take it back.

"Mutilated him. I'm sorry, Yvette."

"Oh, God. My baby."

The look of anguish on her face squeezed Micah. He had to push that aside. He hadn't wanted to trouble this woman, but maybe she needed to know the truth. Maybe this pain was required to ensure justice.

"They weren't supposed to do that," she said. "He told me they would give him something to make him sleep. To make it painless."

"He probably didn't know. Or maybe he knew, but didn't want to trouble you." Micah crossed the room to Yvette and placed his hands on her shoulders as she sobbed. "Yvette, please. Tell me what you know. Help me do something about these awful people who did this to your son."

She shrugged away from his hands and left the room, down a hallway. Micah followed as she shuffled along the carpet and into a side room. A young person's bedroom, something clean and untouched. She lifted a framed picture from the top of a wardrobe. A preteen in a baseball uniform, bat slung over his shoulder. He did look a bit like a young Micah.

"I've kept it the way it was when he lived here. He hasn't been at home since he was fifteen or maybe sixteen. I gave up thinking he would move back in. With the drinking and the drugs… I never knew where he was, most of the time."

"Yvette. Why are they abandoning the casino?"

She clutched the photo to her chest. "Logan owed money. Gambling, drugs, other things… I don't even know. He had worked for the Crossroads people for a couple years, and tried to stop working for them, but he owed too much money. They were going to kill him and me anyway, but then the whole interstate thing happened, and they made him an offer. His life for my life. Make him look like you so they could draw them out."

Micah already knew, but he had to ask. "Draw who out?"

"A drug cartel from down in Mexico. Named the Sina… Sinaliva, Rinalua, or something like that."

His old employers, the Sinaloa. He'd known the cartel had to be involved, but the connection didn't make sense. Something was still missing. "The Crossroads people wanted to collect on a bounty from the cartel."

"No, it wasn't ever about that. Nothing to do with collecting money. It was about I-35."

"What about I-35?"

"The drug cartel, they own the highway from Mexico to

Canada. To move their drugs, I suppose. The Crossroads gang wants to move in on that and control the route."

Realization tickled the back of Micah's neck. "So collecting on this bounty on my head was a ruse the whole time. They want to make the cartel show themselves so Crossroads can start a war with them."

She nodded. "Logan told me the bounty was the only way to get their attention. Harvey and his people are going down to Mexico tomorrow to meet with them. That's where it will happen."

Her face changed, a soft sort of pity pulling it down. "What did you do to these people that they put a price on your head?"

Micah didn't know how to answer. He had testified against them in court, sent many of them to prison. But he didn't see how telling Yvette King that information would help her. She would only see a man who looked like her son, and that fact had indirectly been the cause of her son's brutal murder.

She ran her fingers over the photo frame. "I suppose it doesn't matter."

Micah's time was running out. An impulse to leave now and rush to the casino burned at him. But why? Why should he involve himself in this war between a skinhead gang and a Mexican drug cartel?

Before he could think of an answer to that question, the doorbell rang. From the other room, the dog chirped a single bark.

Yvette gulped. "They're here."

"Who's here?"

"Crossroads. I sent you away yesterday because I knew they would come for me this morning. I wish you would have honored my request, but it's too late now."

Doorbell rang again.

"I thought you made a deal with them," Micah said.

"Logan made a deal with them, but he's gone. They have no reason to stay away anymore."

"If you knew this, then why haven't you left already? Why did you hang around where they knew how to find you?"

She breathed in and out for a few seconds. "Where was I going to go? My son is dead, why does anything have to matter anymore?"

He wanted to argue the point, but he couldn't. Yvette had surrendered.

"You shouldn't have come back," she said. "Now they'll kill you too. I tried to help you, I really did. You should have stayed away."

The front door opened. Yvette dropped the photo frame.

Micah drew his Glock and put a finger to his lips. Grasped Yvette by the hand and guided her out into the hallway, keeping her behind. Pistol out front.

"Hello?" said a sneering voice. "Yvette, are you home?"

She gasped, and Micah chambered a round into the pistol. Inched along the hallway toward the living room.

"Yvette," the voice said, "are you armed back there? You knew we would be here this morning. The fact that you're still here practically gives us license to do this, you know. You pull a gun on me and I'm going to be seriously pissed off."

"He said I would be safe," Yvette babbled. "He said you would leave me alone if he gave himself up to you."

The voice in the living room chuckled. "Come on, Yvette. You had your chance to get out of town. We would have followed you, probably, but you had your chance to make a run for it. This is cause and effect."

Micah paused just before the end of the hallway. He leaned as close as possible without exposing himself. Couldn't see anything except the little dog running laps around the room.

He gritted his teeth and jumped into the living room, pumping the trigger as he landed. He put one bullet in the man's stomach, and another one blasted his shoulder.

The home invader spun, wailing in pain. Micah squeezed off another shot, the screaming bullet puncturing the man's left cheek.

That one did it. He toppled into the television, knocking it over. He collapsed onto the floor, made one last attempt to grasp at the TV stand, then his arms fell to his side. He was silent.

Yvette's dog tore across the room, yipping.

Micah turned to check on Yvette and found himself staring at a hand across her mouth. Attached to that was a man, and in his other hand, he was holding a knife next to Yvette's throat.

# CHAPTER THIRTY-SEVEN

THEY DECIDED TO interrogate the kidnapped gangster at Ethan's place because his garage had overhead beams strong enough to support the guy's weight. Carter lived in an apartment and Rourke's sister was staying with him, so it wasn't much of an argument. Ethan's place was the way to go.

Rourke parked in front of Ethan's house and they popped the trunk to find the gangster wide awake. He shot a foot out and missed Carter's face by a fraction of an inch. Rourke socked him in the jaw and Ethan dragged him out of the trunk. With the three of them working together, it was easy to get him into the garage.

Carter threw a rope over the beam and Rourke tied the mobster's arms together as Ethan held him still. Then, Carter anchored the rope to a workbench and the three of them raised the mobster by his hands so his feet could barely touch the ground.

Rourke's heart pounded in his chest. Murder and kidnapping in a single week. But this was a necessary thing. A good thing.

Ethan kicked off the festivities by punching the mobster in the stomach a few times to soften him up. The mobster kicked and writhed, and he must have been a karate expert or something because his legs whipped out like knives. Rourke got behind him and tied his legs together, and after that, all he could do was wiggle like a worm on a hook.

"You stupid little fucks," the mobster said. "Do you have any idea what you've done? Do you know how much shit is going to rain down on you for doing this?"

Ethan raised his hand to smack him again, but Rourke held his friend back. He waited until the restrained man had calmed down. Once they were all silent, Rourke faced off with him, noting the swastika tattoo on the mobster's forearm. "Why the swastika? Why believe in something based on such hate and ignorance?"

The mobster's chest heaved a few times, then a grin spread across his face. "It's not a belief, it's the truth. Pure societies always function better. This mixed-race experiment the United States has been running for the last couple hundred years is a total failure." He flicked his head toward Ethan. "Your Christ-killing friend here and his people have been run out of every country they've ever lived in since the beginning of time. Why do you think that is?"

Ethan growled and cracked the mobster with a right

hook so fierce that Rourke feared he might have broken the man's jaw. He had to pull Ethan away because it wouldn't do much good to kill their prisoner before he'd said anything useful.

"Dude," Carter said. "We don't give a shit about your political leanings. We want info about the casino. How many guards, where is the money kept, is it in a safe, what's the combination. How many of you will be there tomorrow night?"

"Start talking," Rourke said.

The man spit blood onto the concrete floor of the garage. "Why would I do that?"

Rourke took his hunting knife and flicked it across the mobster's face, giving him a diagonal slash under his eye. "Because you can die here, right now, or you can tell us what we want to know."

The mobster laughed. "You dumb fucks. You're too late. You walk in there tomorrow, it'll all be over."

A cold chill hit Rourke's spine. "What will be over?"

"If you'd tried to rob us a week ago, you would've had almost no trouble. We were too busy planning our move against the Sinaloa."

Ethan slugged the mobster in the kidney. "The *what*? What the hell is a Sinaloa?"

"The Mexican cartel, you dumbshit. We were going to shut down the casino and go south. But now that things have changed and they're coming here today, none of that matters. They figured out what we were up to, so we had to change the plan. They thought they could catch us with our pants down, but they underestimated Crossroads. We'll be ready and waiting to tear them to pieces."

"I don't understand," Rourke said. "Your gang was going on a trip south and now you're not? What does this have to do with us?"

The mobster spat more blood onto the floor. "You can try your little robbery operation *today*, but you're going to walk into a full-scale war, right there in the Dort Mall. We're going to surprise those fuckers before they can surprise us.

"So it doesn't matter where we keep the money or how many of the pit bosses are strapped. Everyone in the whole damn Crossroads organization, from Harvey to the low-level muscle guys are going to be armed with automatic weapons and defending the mall today, and then tomorrow, we'll all be gone. Disappeared and setting up shop somewhere else. You're not going to see a dime of that cash, you idiots."

Rourke gritted his teeth. He couldn't accept this if it were true. All those months of planning, of acquiring weapons and ammunition, of staking out the casino entrances and exits... all wasted because the timing was off.

Such a little detail that could make a huge difference.

Rourke opened his mouth to question the mobster further, but he was interrupted when the door to the house creaked open. Into the garage slinked a beautiful redhead, followed by a tall man. Both them with silenced guns in hand. Cartoonishly long. They were dressed in dark suits, like government agents on TV shows.

Ethan was standing directly in front of the workbench where he'd left his pistol. Ethan tried to spin and snatch it, but the woman raised her gun. Pulled back the slide.

"Ethan, don't," Rourke said.

"Listen to him, Ethan," the woman said. "We didn't come here to kill you, just to talk. I don't want to pull this trigger. But believe me when I say that I won't take that chance with you. I've seen your rap sheet."

Rourke and Carter gathered closer to Ethan on one side of the garage, opposite the woman and man. The secured gangster hung limply from the overhead beam, his eyes flicking back and forth between the two parties.

"What are you doing with this individual?" she said.

"None of your business," Rourke said.

The woman pivoted and shot the gangster in the forehead. The silencer on her gun made the blast seem like a whip crack instead of the thunderous crash it would have been in this small space.

The gangster's head slumped forward, blood pouring onto the floor.

"Why would you do such an imbecilic thing?" Carter said, flailing his hands in the air. "He had information."

"You were going to have to kill him anyway," she said. "If you let him go, you'd be dead within minutes. Plus, good chance he was lying about whatever he told you."

"Who are you?" Rourke said.

"Don't tell him," the man in the suit said.

The woman shrugged and addressed her partner. "What do I care?" Then to Rourke: "I'm Olivia, and this is my colleague Jeremy."

Jeremy took a hand off his gun to offer a brief wave, then resumed pointing it directly at Ethan's head.

"What do you want?" Rourke said.

"We know who you are," Olivia said. "We know what you're trying to do at the Dort Mall. We came here, tonight, to politely ask you not to break into that casino. Maybe you heard about that dead body they altered to look like someone else?"

Rourke knew exactly who they were talking about. He wondered if Olivia had already figured out they'd met the guy who looked like Logan King. Probably, since she knew so much about everything else.

"That was all about starting a war," Olivia said. "The gang is packing up to head south and face off with the Sinaloa cartel tomorrow, and we need to make sure you don't mess that up. We have orders to apprehend some high-ranking Sinaloa people, and they don't come out of hiding often."

"That's the thing," Rourke said. "It's not happening that way."

Olivia narrowed her eyes. "What do you mean?"

Rourke gestured at the dead gangster, his limp weight slowly oscillating back and forth on the rope. "Right before you came in, he was telling us something. Maybe he would have told us more if you hadn't shot him."

She sighed and bit her lower lip. Sneaked a glance at the

dead gangster, blood dribbling out of the hole in his fore-head. "My mistake. What did he say?"

"Why should we tell you anything?" Ethan said.

Jeremy chambered a round into his gun.

Rourke held his hands out. "The cartel is coming here. Today. The war is happening in Michigan, not in Mexico."

Olivia and Jeremy shared a look of surprise. This was new information to them, obviously.

"Shit," she said to her colleague. "We aren't ready to go yet."

An idea popped into Rourke's head. It was sloppy, impulsive, and most likely, destined to fail. But it did put the odds back in his favor. These two looked like they knew how to handle themselves.

"What if we team up?" he said.

Olivia narrowed her eyes. "Why would we do that?"

"Because if Crossroads and the cartel are warring, they're going to be out in the mall, not in the basement where the casino is. We sneak in the back, get the money, and then work our way out, and we'll provide guns to help you. You-watch-our-back, we-watch-yours kind of thing."

She pursed her lips. "But we don't care about your little casino robbery."

"We could cut you in," Rourke said.

"Damn it, guys," Ethan said under his breath, "we shouldn't be making deals with these people."

For a second, Olivia seemed to consider Rourke's offer. Then, the gangster hanging from the beam jerked. Like a spastic shudder running up his torso and into his arms. Some kind of last gasp or muscle reaction.

It was enough to get the attention of Olivia and Jeremy. They both reacted and swung their weapons toward the gangster. In a flash, Ethan snatched the pistol off the workbench, shot Jeremy in the chest, and then Olivia in the head. The non-silenced pistol blasted like a rocket taking off in the small space of this garage.

Jeremy didn't go down, so Ethan shot him again.

It all happened too quickly for Rourke to do anything to prevent it. One second, he was making a deal. The next, spent pistol casings jangled on the concrete and these two strangers were crumpling to the floor.

"Son of a bitch," Rourke said as he gazed at the bodies of the two people breathing their last breaths in Ethan's garage. Three dead people within ten feet of him. "What did you do that for?"

"You heard her," Ethan said. "They don't care about getting into the casino. It's all about some gang war power play thing. They said they just came to talk, but why would they let us walk out of here? Why tell us their names and their plans if they were going to let us live?"

Rourke had to admit that Ethan had a point. "Doesn't matter now. Get their guns and get ready. We'll come back later and deal with these bodies. Right now, we're going back to the mall, while we still have time."

## CHAPTER THIRTY-EIGHT

MICAH WATCHED YVETTE'S eyes as she struggled not to move, since she had a knife pressed to her neck. The blade made a slight indentation in her skin, but her assailant wasn't holding it tight enough to draw blood. Only enough to keep her in place.

The man standing behind Yvette tilted his head to look around her. Micah recognized him. The same bushy-eyebrowed man who had given him the password in the basement of the mall, his passage into the casino.

Counterfeit.

"Hello," Bushy Eyebrows said as his teeth gritted in an angry sneer of a smile. "You again. I had a feeling we weren't done with you."

"Let her go."

"You know I can't do that. Harvey doesn't like to leave witnesses. Your time is up too, Mr. Reed. I wasn't sure

238

when I saw you before, but now that you've dropped the phony contacts and glasses, I am. It's good that I ran into you."

Micah had to do some quick math. The knife was at her throat. He was five feet away. He couldn't rush at Bushy Eyebrows quickly enough to disarm him. But enough of his head was exposed from behind Yvette that if Micah could get the Glock up in time, he could put a bullet in Bushy Eyebrows' forehead, maybe before he could react and kill Yvette.

Maybe. Or he might accidentally shoot Yvette if he wasn't careful.

Her eyes were wide open. Full of panic. Even though she'd known they would come for her, that fact probably wasn't a comfort right now, facing fate. Micah was the only person standing between her and certain death.

Bushy Eyebrows flinched and Micah lifted the weapon. No time to think, just to act.

Too slow.

The knife sliced across Yvette's throat, digging in and carving a line. The gash immediately turned red as blood poured out. Bushy Eyebrows heaved her body at Micah, then turned to escape out the way he'd come. He managed to spin all the way around before Micah got his finger on the trigger.

Micah leaned to the right, aimed his gun, and shot the man in the back, all before Yvette tumbled into his arms. She landed on him, knocking Micah back a few steps. He felt dampness on the front of his shirt as her arms flopped around him. She was gasping for breath, gulping blood down.

He lowered her to the ground while keeping his eyes on Bushy Eyebrows. The man didn't move. He was sprawled with his head to the side, eyes open. Not blinking. Micah waited a couple of seconds to be sure that he couldn't detect any rise and fall of Bushy Eyebrows' chest.

Micah turned Yvette on her back, and he took her hand and placed it over the hole in her throat. Pressed her hand down to close up the wound.

"Yvette, listen to me. You're going to be okay. You're going to make it through this. Just stay awake, and I'm going to get you to a hospital."

Blood continued to pour out.

"You have to press hard. As hard as you can."

Her eyes darted back and forth. Despite forcing her hand down to put pressure on the wound, blood still leaked from it in pulsing waves. Trickled between her fingers, turning her hand into a red mess.

She tried to speak, but a trickle of blood dribbled out of the side of her mouth instead. She stilled and her eyes blinked, and then shut. The blood continued to leak, but her mouth stopped moving.

He held her for another minute, brain swimming. So much chaos. Micah had killed two people in the last two minutes. And he'd let another one die because he hadn't been quick enough to save her.

Could he have saved her? Had it even been possible?

None of that mattered right now. He had to get out of here before others came to look for her.

He let go of Yvette, and then noticed a perfect bloody thumbprint on her temple. His thumbprint. He smudged it and thought about what else he might have touched in this house. Front door, for sure. Had he handled anything in Logan's room? He couldn't remember.

This woman on the floor hadn't done anything wrong. She'd been the victim of a terrible bargain her son had engineered, and now they were both dead because of it.

She deserved justice.

"I'm not going to let them get away with this."

He checked the gangster he'd shot in the back to ensure he was dead, then Micah hurried into Logan's room to check for fingerprints. Made his way back to the living room, keeping his gun on the man there. Still not moving.

He wiped off both sides of the front doorknob, then paused when Yvette's dog darted out from under the couch. Glared up at him.

"I'm really sorry about your mom, but you can't stay here, dog."

The dog cocked its little head but didn't move.

"No one is coming to feed you anymore."

The dog still didn't move.

Micah snatched the dog by the collar and dragged it—yipping and biting—out the front door. He slammed the door behind him so the dog couldn't get back in, then he released the collar. The dog stared up at him again, whining.

"I'm serious, buddy. Someone else is going to have to take you because I don't even live here. So go now, be brave. You can do this."

The dog sat on the porch. Then plopped onto its belly, panting and sour-faced.

Micah didn't have time for this. After he had convinced himself the dog would be fine, he left the porch and jumped in the rental car. Sped through the streets of Burton to rejoin the interstate. One thing on his mind: getting to that casino before Crossroads had a chance to finish packing and leave to start a war with the Sinaloa. By tomorrow, they would all be gone.

After a couple minutes on the interstate, he yanked his phone out of his pocket and called Frank's hospital room. He spent so long on hold, he was only a mile or two away from the mall by the time they'd connected him with Frank's room.

"Frank."

"Yeah, kid. What's up?" Frank sounded groggy, gravelly, not like himself.

"Everything has changed. I found the mother of the lookalike they killed. It wasn't about a bounty at all. These Crossroads people were trying to draw out the cartel so they could start a war. They're headed down to Mexico tomorrow so they can kill all the head Sinaloa players. They want to move drugs up and down I-35 without worrying about cartel interference."

Frank coughed a bit. "Not about the bounty. Actually, that makes a lot of sense."

"If they're leaving, I don't have much time to put a stop to all of this. I'm on my way back to the mall right now to intervene. I'm almost there."

"Why?"

Micah stopped short, stumbled over his words. "What do you mean?"

"This was never about you. Your part is done here. You found out who this kid was, and that's what we set out to do. And if they're trying to start a war, maybe you let them. You have no stake in that war."

"But it's so much bigger than that. These people have to be stopped. Logan King needs justice."

"So what are you going to do? Waltz in there and take on the whole neo-Nazi army? Think this through, Micah. You overestimate your power in this situation."

Micah held the phone away from his ear. As he neared the mall, he saw lights flickering near the building, above the trees that obscured his view. Flashes like fireworks, maybe. But that wasn't likely since it wasn't dark outside.

"I gotta go, Frank."

Micah turned into the parking lot to find a row of cars beyond the trees. And a line of people in front of those cars.

And the source of the lights: automatic weapons fire.

# CHAPTER THIRTY-NINE

THE AK-47 and extra ammo weighed Rourke down like a suit of armor. The gangster they'd held hostage in Ethan's garage had told the truth. There was a full-scale epic battle occurring on the front side of the mall. Rourke couldn't see it firsthand from behind the mall, but he didn't need to. Sounded like a Hollywood war movie.

As he and his two friends hustled through the trees behind the back side of the mall, he didn't care about excess noise attracting attention. With the constant gunfire eruptions, they clearly didn't need to make a stealthy approach.

But they could make use of all this chaos, hopefully. Sneak in the back amid a frontal assault, get to the cashier, get the money, get the hell out. This ambush development was the best thing that had happened to the plan since they'd started. Instead of facing a basement full of casino guards, they would probably walk into an empty room.

An empty room with a shitload of money in it. Life-changing money.

Ethan paused at the edge of the parking lot, put his hand on the dumpster's corner. He leaned over, wheezing.

"You okay?" Rourke said.

"Fine. I just need a minute."

"We don't have a minute," Carter said. "Who knows how long this is going to last. The cops will be here momentarily, and we need to be done and gone before they show up."

Ethan waved a hand in the general direction of the crackling weapons fire coming from the front of the mall. "Do you really think with a massive gang war going on, that the cops are what we need to worry about?"

Carter opened his mouth to reply, but Rourke held up a hand. "Ethan, can you rest later? We really do need to hurry. If not for the cops, we need to worry about some of those people breaking through and coming downstairs. Let's get in there while it's probably empty. It's too good to pass up."

Ethan nodded, and they hustled across the parking lot, assault rifles and pockets full of rounds clanking.

They skidded to a stop at the back door, all of them now panting. Rourke's hands vibrated and his breakfast bounced around his stomach like basketballs on a trampoline.

"You have the kit, right?" Rourke said to Carter. "Tell me you have the kit."

Carter pulled a small cardboard box out of his pocket. "Next day shipping, motherfucker," he said with a smirk. Carter was actually enjoying this. Or he was working overtime to cover up his fears.

He pulled out a set of tools from the box, then held them in the palm of his hand. "I think this is all of them."

Rourke closely examined the tools. Looked like a collection of dentist picks. "You remember how to do this, right?"

Carter frowned. "I think so. I mean, I watched that Micah guy do it, so I think I can too. Didn't seem that intricate. The bendy one goes in the bottom, and the curvy one goes in the top. Then you jiggle until the shit opens."

Carter leaned down to the back door. The area was shaded, so Rourke took out his phone and shined the flashlight app onto the keyhole.

Ethan hunkered down, assault rifle pointed at the ground in front of the door. His eyes were laser-focused, his mouth pulled into a sneer. Air whistled in and out of his flared nostrils.

He shoved a mag into the AK-47.

Like the sudden rush of cold when jumping into a pool, the full weight of adrenaline and anxiety hit Rourke. In all of his previous years put together, he'd had a total of two guns pointed at him. Seen one dead body. This week alone, he'd seen four people die in front of him. He'd killed one himself, and his best friend had killed two others.

That qualified as a "mass" killing, didn't it?

Rourke swayed on his feet. The sweat on his palms made the phone slip, and he bobbled it in the air.

"Keep the light steady," Carter said.

The door burst open, knocking Carter back. At the top of the stairs stood a man in a pinstripe suit with a streak of blood running down his temple. His face had been a mess of panic, but it quickly morphed into confusion at the sight of these three standing outside the back door of the mall.

The casino was not empty. Activity, in the form of voices and gunfire, emanated from down those stairs.

Ethan raised his assault rifle and jerked the trigger, putting three holes in the man's gut. The rifle blasts were like bombs so close to Rourke's ears, and the flash of light momentarily blinded him.

His vision returned as the man in the pinstripe suit tumbled back down the stairs and the door started to shut.

"Door!" Rourke shouted.

Carter reached out and grabbed hold of it, barely managing to catch it before it closed. "I guess I can check about getting my money back for the lockpicks, eh?"

"I thought you said it would be empty," Ethan said.

"I was hoping it would be," Rourke said. "Doesn't matter now. We have weapons and access, and it's not going to get any better than this."

He realized this raid was maybe the last stupid thing he would ever get to do in his life. And that he didn't care anymore. As long as his friends were with him, this was going to happen.

They were finally going to right the wrongs.

He gripped his assault rifle. "Okay. Time to get paid."

Before Micah had a chance to grasp what was happening, someone in the line of attackers turned and shot at his car. A few bullets punctured the grille and the front hood. He ducked. Quick hands snatched his compact Glock.

Had a split second thought about Frank not getting his deposit back for the rental. Boba Fett reminded him to focus or he'd drown in a puddle of his own blood inside this rental car.

A bullet cracked the windshield, and a second barrage blew it out. Glass sprinkled his back. His ears filled with a sound like the crinkling of fancy gift wrapping paper. Then, he felt the car sink a few inches as the front tires deflated. He wasn't driving out of here, and if he stayed in this car, he'd be dead in less than a minute. It's not as if the car rental company had offered a bulletproof upgrade.

Micah reached up to tug on his seatbelt and felt a bullet whiz past his hand. Yanked it back down. The buckle was pinned underneath him.

An idea formed.

He stashed the gun in his waistband and popped open the glove box. Took out a pocket knife and the car's manual, which must have weighed at least a couple pounds. He had to pray it would be heavy enough.

A shaky hand turned the key in the ignition, and the car grumbled to life. He cut through the seatbelt with the pocket knife and opened the passenger door. Gulped a quick breath, then dropped the manual on the gas pedal and jumped out of the passenger side as the car began to accelerate toward the line of attackers.

Whoever was shooting focused their fire on the moving car, and Micah got to his feet and sprinted with all his might toward the back parking lot. His feet barely touched the ground.

As he ran, he sneaked a look at the mall. Opposite the men shooting at it, another line of people returned fire. Casino employees, judging by the dark suits. They had pushed bits and pieces of the Dort Mall decorations to form a barricade behind the windows. Pinball machines and airplane parts and other bits of junk, stacked to provide cover from weapons fire. The Crossroads gang had prepared for this attack. They weren't planning on traveling south, so that meant the ones shooting had to be Sinaloa.

Micah kept running, but he squinted to identify the men firing at the mall. His eyes landed on a particular person. A familiar face.

Micah's heart pulsed, stopped, sped up.

Couldn't be him. But it was.

He was looking at Gustavo Salazar, one of Micah's former employers. Deep scar across his forehead, like a thick and wavy wrinkle. A man who had somehow escaped prosecution from the feds, and now here he stood, in Michigan, engaged in a war with some skinhead gang.

A shootout in a mall parking lot in broad daylight. That the Sinaloa would have the balls to do such a thing reminded Micah how insanely dangerous they were.

Micah willed his legs to sprint faster. He'd be hidden by the corner of the mall in three or four more seconds. Getting there would solve his most immediate problem. But, even if he could escape the parking lot, they were here. If they had seen his face, they would know for sure that he was alive now. Two years of living in Denver under an assumed name, and now, one look over at this man would ruin everything.

They would kill him. Probably after days or weeks of torture, if only to make themselves feel a little better about how he'd betrayed them. They would also come for Frank and then Micah's family. The Sinaloa wouldn't stop until everyone he'd known had been eradicated in the most heinous ways possible.

Micah held up a hand to the side of his face to obscure it.

Just before he turned the corner to the side of the mall, he glanced back one more time, and Gustavo was leading two of his men on a charge toward the same corner of the mall. Gustavo's men were carrying automatic weapons. Micah's pistol wasn't much of a match for that.

Had they seen him? Or were they chasing what they thought was some random casino employee trying to escape?

Micah rounded the side and hugged the outer mall wall as he approached the back lot. His chest burned from the exertion. He hadn't run this hard in years, but fearing for your life will do that to you.

When he turned the back corner, he spotted the three casino robbers, standing outside the open back door of the mall. Gustavo had to be less than fifty paces behind him. Micah couldn't make it to the trees at the edge of the lot fast enough. But he could reach Rourke and his gang.

They could help him.

"Wait!" he shouted at the three of them. "Wait, please."

Micah could barely make out his expression with the blinding sun overhead, but he thought he'd seen Rourke smile.

Ethan raised an AK-47, but Rourke put his hand on top of it, pushing it down as Micah neared them.

"You're just in time," Rourke said.

Micah could barely catch his breath. "You're not actually going to rob the casino now, are you?"

"Fuck yeah, we are," Carter said.

"You can help," Rourke said.

Micah was about to protest when bullets whizzed by from behind. Gustavo and his men had caught up. Micah didn't argue anymore. If he didn't disappear immediately, he'd be spotted. Shot to death.

He and his three new heist companions dashed through the door, down the stairs, into the casino.

# CHAPTER FORTY

ROURKE HOPPED OVER the body of the dead man in the pinstriped suit, with Carter, Ethan, and Micah trailing. With each step down the long and dark stairwell and into the casino, his heart's relentless thumping increased speed. He hadn't been here since he was a kid; not since his father had squandered what little money they had so he could get his adrenaline fix.

Breathing this same casino air didn't make him feel little again, as he'd worried it might. He did recognize the sour smell of cigar smoke and the hint of liquor floating into his nostrils.

Near the bottom of the stairs, he noticed the absence of light on the casino floor, but gun blasts flashed across the room like a lazy strobe light. The constant rattle of gunfire boxed Rourke's ears.

This room was supposed to be empty. It was definitely

not. He'd entertained fantasies of strutting into a barren room, free to take the cash at will, not having to pull a trigger even once.

But he and his friends were walking into a death trap, and he knew it. And even though he was aware of that, and even though his heart raced, Rourke didn't feel like turning around to leave. He wanted to push on, to fight through the guards and get what he came for.

A pair of legs came into view at the bottom of the stairs. Rourke pointed his AK-47 and squeezed the trigger. The weapon jerked like a rabid dog in his hands, the recoil naturally trying to elevate the barrel after the shot. He'd have to get used to that.

His bullet poked a hole in the man's thigh and he tumbled forward. Someone had been shooting at him, and bullets peppered the bottom three steps. One bullet tore a hole in that man's head, splattering gray and red chunks nearby.

A piece of scalp with brown hair landed on the bottom stair, and Rourke couldn't help but gawk at it. He didn't want to, but couldn't look away. So utterly disgusting.

A hand gripped Rourke's shoulder, and it broke his concentration. He couldn't hear anything over the gunfire.

Carter leaned forward and shouted above the fray. "We need to think about this. We don't have any way to conceal our entrance. We'll be vulnerable as soon as we step into view."

Rourke nodded. They were still hidden by the stairwell,

four or five steps away from emerging into view of whoever was in the room.

Carter put his lips right next to Rourke's ear. "We are at a serious disadvantage here, as soon as we leave these stairs."

Before Rourke could answer, his body jerked to the side as Ethan knocked him out of the way. The big guy was hopping down the stairs, two at a time, his mouth open and an inaudible war cry bellowing from his lips.

Ethan landed at the bottom of the stairs and squeezed off a volley of assault rifle fire in all directions. He pumped out thirty rounds in three or four seconds. Light from the gunfire flashed up the stairwell like headlights in a dark tunnel.

Rourke didn't have time to think. He had to help his friend. He grabbed Carter's shirt and tugged him the rest of the way down. Rourke craned his neck and found Micah still halfway up the stairs, looking up at the closed back door. His gun out and pointed into the darkness. Must have been expecting whoever had been chasing him to burst through that door.

Whatever. If Micah didn't want to help, he could expect to be cut out of a share of the casino money. And if he got in the way, he'd face even more severe consequences.

They'd entered life-or-death territory. Everything else was useless.

As Rourke hit the ground, he couldn't see anything at first. Smoke filled the room. Gunshots rang in his ears.

Ethan was still firing, and Carter lifted his rifle and squeezed off a few shots.

Rourke's eyes adjusted a little, even though they were already starting to burn from the smoke. When he moved his feet, poker chips scattered.

He could see a line of slot machines in the middle of the room. Two of the poker tables near that line had been turned over, and a couple heads were poking out from behind them. Some flickering light source flared at the far end of the room, but he couldn't tell what it was.

He and his two friends were standing out in the open, at the bottom of the stairwell.

Rourke snatched his friends by their arms and dragged them a couple feet to the left so they were partially blocked behind a table covered with green felt. Poker or Blackjack, hard to tell. He lifted his AK and squinted through the smoke. Saw a gangly man try to run from a poker table to a slot machine.

Rourke aimed and pulled the trigger. Once, twice, three times, all controlled single-shot bursts. He was getting better at this already.

The gangly man made it to the slot machine, and then he leaned out, jerking his gun's trigger. The bullets didn't come anywhere close, though. He must not have been able to see well either, through all the smoke.

Rourke lined up the sight and squeezed again, and this time, the man flew backward and stumbled into a dormant slot machine. Big *crack* as his head connected with metal and glass.

The shooting ceased inside the room. He could hear it coming from nearby in several directions, but the room had gone quiet. Rourke could now see the source of the light in the far corner of the room. A fire was quivering and growing taller. Hard to see what was burning, but it didn't look too serious. Not yet, at least.

"They can't be gone," Carter said amid the quiet. His chest hitched as he breathed.

The smoke cleared a bit, but it was still hard to see the full scope of the room. "Most of them are probably upstairs, dealing with the attack on the front of the mall. Holding them off." Rourke pointed his gun at the fire at the opposite end. "We might need to worry about that fire, though."

"Then we gotta move," Ethan said, mouth in a snarl.

Rourke followed him toward the cashier's cage in the near corner. In their path: broken card tables, mountains of chips, overturned chairs. Dead bodies, some still leaking blood out onto the carpet.

Rustling came behind a slot machine near the middle of the room. Fifty feet away.

"Come out," Ethan said as he pointed his AK in that direction. "Come on out of there. Real slow, and let me see your hands. Do not mess with me."

A pair of hands emerged from behind the slot machine. A pistol gripped in one.

Rourke raised his weapon. "Drop the gun, asshole."

The gun went clattering to the ground, and the hands turned into arms, then a person stepped into view. A kid, couldn't have been more than eighteen or nineteen. He was wearing a card dealer's green visor. Shaking, terrified.

The kid opened his mouth, but a burst of gunfire interrupted him. Ethan's AK-47 spit a volley of bullets at him, punching holes from his stomach to his head. The kid sank to his knees, gasped, then fell flat on his face. Blood immediately seeped into the carpet in a circle, spreading out from his chest.

"Jesus, dude," Carter said. "He was just a kid."

Ethan growled. "If he works here, he's a Nazi shitbag like the rest. I'm going to kill every one of them I can. I don't want to hear about your humanitarian bullshit right now."

"Humanitarian?" Carter said. "There's a difference between—"

Rourke snapped his fingers, which was still a faint sound compared to the gunshots rumbling above. He didn't want to dwell on Ethan's bloodlust, and he didn't want Ethan to think about it, either. "Guys. Focus."

They proceeded to the cashier's cage, a small room with a cutout window protected by bars. The door to the cage was locked.

"You got the lockpicks?" Rourke said to Carter.

Carter dipped a hand into his back pocket, then his face went white. Shook his head. "Sorry, I don't have them. I dropped them in the parking lot."

"Shit," Ethan said.

Carter pouted. "What do you want from me? They

were shooting at us, and with the door already open, we didn't need them. Should I go out the back and look?"

Rourke remembered the three men who had been chasing Micah. They might still be out there. "No, don't do that."

Ethan lifted his AK at the door, but Carter stopped him.

"Wait," Carter said. "There might be some kind of trap or something if you shoot off that lock. You might set off one of those blue paint bombs that ruins all the money."

Rourke stared at the door. Carter was probably right. A wave of disappointment so severe gripped him, that for a moment he experienced an overpowering urge to sit. Let this roadblock overcome him and give up.

To come this close and then fail?

An idea appeared. He turned back to the stairs. "Micah? Are you still there?"

# CHAPTER FORTY-ONE

ICAH HEARD HIS name, but the voice didn't register at first. He'd been eye-locked in a staring contest with that back door of the mall, waiting for Gustavo to come bursting through. His Glock pointed up the stairs into the abyss, waiting for a chance to punch a hole in that bastard's head.

"Why didn't I try for the trees?" he mused. "I should have tried for the trees instead of trapping myself down here."

He probably wouldn't have made it to the edge of the parking lot unharmed, but there'd been a chance. He'd made a choice now, and couldn't go back.

Still, the door above had not opened.

Why hadn't that door opened?

Maybe Gus had hoped someone in the basement level would take Micah out. Or he was standing outside that door, waiting for Micah to realize the only way out was to venture back up those stairs. Or maybe Gus had already died in a firefight. Or possibly, Gus hadn't seen him at all. Maybe he hadn't recognized Michael McBriar, the man who'd sold out his people in exchange for Witness Protection.

There was no way to know without walking up the stairs and opening that door. Without exposing himself.

"Micah?" came a voice from below.

Micah snapped out of his trance and descended the stairs. Most of the casino was shrouded in a foggy haze. A few emergency lights illuminated some sections, but most of the room was dim. A bit of smoke hung in the air and a small fire lit up the far corner of the room.

Dead bodies had stacked on top of each other like leaves covering a lawn. The air stank. There had to be three dozen dead here, maybe more.

Carter, Ethan, and Rourke were standing in front of the cashier's room in the corner, pointing their guns at it.

Micah lowered his pistol and joined them. "What?"

"Can you break into this room?" Rourke said.

Micah glanced back at the stairs.

"Help us, and we'll help you," Rourke said. "We'll all fight our way out of here together."

The main door to the casino burst open, and three men rushed in. Not casino employees. Dressed in dark clothes from head to toe, these were cartel men. Had to be. Micah couldn't see their faces in the rush, but he knew his own kind. They moved with liquid speed, fanning out and deftly navigating the mess of the room.

With nothing in the immediate area to hide behind, Rourke and the others lifted their assault rifles and started firing. The blasts were deafening. Micah crouched and took aim at the legs of a man running at full speed, spitting two quick shots, and the second hit the man in the kneecap. He twisted and bounced against a slot machine. Fell to the ground. Micah aimed and shot him in the head.

Through the gray haze, Micah couldn't make out his face. He didn't know if he would have recognized the man, anyway. The cartel must have been mostly new members at this point.

Then, he spent a split second thinking about how easy killing had once again become. The way violence became natural in the cartel when he drank every night to drown the actions of that day. As much as he'd wanted to leave that old person behind like a bulky couch in a vacated apartment, it was still him.

He was still a killer, and always would be.

Micah snapped out of it when one of Rourke's guys screamed. He looked up to see Ethan clutching his arm. AK-47 on the ground. Carter jumped in front of him to act as a shield and launched a round of bullets in an arc.

The men on the other side of the room stopped coming. One of them fell in a heap, and the other spun into a roulette table. Both of them, dead.

Ethan backed into the wall and slid down with a grunt. He removed his hand from the wound, revealing a bloody mess of a forearm. Carter took a few steps toward the newly-dead men, his assault rifle out in front while Rourke dropped to his knees and helped put pressure on Ethan's wound.

Reminded Micah of applying pressure to Yvette King's throat wound, and how she bled out anyway. He couldn't do anything to stop it. She'd been fated to die before he'd ever met her.

*Focus, Micah. Focus.*

"Shit. It hurts," said Ethan.

"Can you stand?" Rourke said.

Ethan growled. "Give me a minute."

"Micah," Rourke said, pleading. "Get us in that room, please. We need to hurry this up."

Micah could now clearly see the fire in the corner of the room. A long table was engulfed in flames, starting to spread to the wall. They needed to be out of here in about five minutes, before that fire either engulfed the whole room, or it became too smoky to breathe.

He examined the lock, then realized it didn't matter. His lock picking tools were back in Denver, in a drawer in the kitchen of his condo. "Do you have tools?"

Rourke, his hands still gripping Ethan's bleeding arm, shook his head.

"A screwdriver? Needle-nose pliers? Fucking paper clips?"

Carter backed up toward them, his eyes still on the front door. "We don't have anything."

Ethan grunted, and Micah could see he was flicking his head at something on a table. A woman, sprawled, her chest a red curtain of blood.

Micah had a feeling he knew what Ethan was implying, and he got up to check. She had long hair, and he expected he'd find bobby pins tying it back. As he neared her, he felt his stomach twist in knots. She was pretty—or she had been. Below the table lay a collection of broken glass. Waitress. She was probably serving drinks to gamblers at the moment the Sinaloa men broke in, took a bullet in the chest, found herself dying on the table, wondering why.

Micah's breath caught in his throat.

He recognized her. The girl who'd first approached him when he'd come to the casino to search for Frank. The girl whose brow had knitted in worry when Micah was being questioned by Harvey and his goons. This girl who had parents, and siblings, and probably a boyfriend, all of whom would cry at her funeral. Would wonder what they could have done differently to change the course of her life.

Micah reached out, his hand shaking. He didn't want to touch this dead girl. He couldn't see well in the dim light, so he had to dig through her hair. It was soft, recently conditioned.

But he found what he was looking for. Two bobby pins on the side of her head. He plucked them out and stumbled back toward the cashier cage.

"You okay?" Rourke said.

Micah didn't answer him, instead broke one bobby pin in half, then knelt in front of the door. He inserted it a quarter of an inch in the bottom of the lock, then bent it and applied pressure. The other half, he bent so it had a curved tip, then inserted it into the top of the lock and went to work, digging it around, feeling for the pins.

"Will this take long?" Carter said.

"Bobby pins aren't ideal. Maybe a minute or two."

Above their heads, muted gun blasts raged on. Micah wondered if any of the mall employees had died in the assault. Maybe the hockey store staff all possessed guns of their own and had joined in the chaos.

"If you think you can't open it, let me know," Rourke said. "We're running out of time."

"I can get this," Micah said, and he felt a click on the inside of the lock. Good. He dug further to hit the next pin, and it clicked instantly. He twisted the lower bobby pin, and the lock turned.

"You did it," Rourke said.

Ethan snatched up his AK-47 and staggered to his feet. Blood still oozing from the wound on his arm.

Micah swung open the door, and the three casino robbers readied their weapons.

But they found no armed guards inside.

Just a middle-aged woman, cowering in the corner, tears streaming down her face. Her hands were thrust out in front of her, holding a knife. The blade jittered and glinted in the dim light.

"Where's the money?" Carter said.

The woman said nothing. Micah noticed a collection of lockboxes around her, all of them open and empty.

"Where is the damn money?" Ethan said, raising his rifle at her.

Micah stepped in front of Ethan, shielding the woman from his rifle. "It's not here, is it?"

The woman shook her head. "Harvey came and took it all. He's in his office. His office says *maintenance* outside of it." She tilted her head behind her. "Can I please go now? I don't want to die here."

"You should probably stay here," Rourke said. "Keep your head down and don't say anything. You can leave out the back door in a few minutes."

Ethan stormed out of the cage and through the room. Fire in his eyes and a sneer on his face.

"Wait," Rourke said, and they all hustled after the big guy. Ethan's heavy feet stomped along the carpet. He didn't bother maneuvering around the dead bodies, he marched directly toward the maintenance room.

Micah struggled to keep up, navigating the obstacles of overturned tables and haphazard chairs in his way. Ten feet ahead of him, Ethan reached the door, kicked it open, and his head snapped back as he took a bullet in the face.

# CHAPTER FORTY-TWO

A  S ETHAN'S ARMS pinwheeled and he tumbled backward, Micah watched the whole thing in slow motion. The spurt of blood ejecting from Ethan's temple in a broken arc. The way his knees buckled while he fell, as if he were folding in half.

He collapsed on his back, dead eyes pointed straight at the ceiling. Micah hadn't known Ethan, and had actually found him to be a surly bastard. But he felt the devastation he could see on Rourke's and Carter's faces.

For a moment, no one did anything. Muted gunfire rattled above their heads on the above-ground level of the mall. Rourke and Carter stared.

The silence broke when Rourke bolted to the edge of the door, pushing his body next to the frame. He pointed the nose of his AK-47 into the room and blasted inside at full auto as he swung the stock in a circle. Screaming at the top of his lungs.

The thumping of bullets lasted only two seconds.

"Are you dead?" Rourke said as he slammed a fresh magazine into his rifle. "Are you dead in there, Harvey, you racist piece of garbage?"

Silence came back from the room. Micah inched toward the open door, trying to get a look inside. When he'd come close enough, he spotted a body in a plush leather chair, leaning back. He raised his pistol and took a step into the doorway. The same man he'd seen in the casino. Harvey, the owner.

"He's dead," Micah said.

Carter had been kneeling by Ethan's body, which had gone still. Carter leaned forward, his long blond hair sprawled out over Ethan's chest like a mop. His back was hitching. Crying.

"Ethan is gone," Rourke said.

Carter lifted his head, tears streaming down his face. "How could they kill my best friend? They shot him right in the head like some kind of lame horse. How could they do that?"

Rourke's lip jutted out and he blinked, fighting back tears. "I know, buddy. But we don't have time right now. Please, let's get this over with and we'll deal with that later."

Carter and Rourke joined Micah in the maintenance room. Harvey had slumped in the leather chair, with stacks of cash in front of him. Hundreds of thousands in bills piled up like a year's worth of unread mail.

Micah hadn't seen so much cash in one place in a long

time. This kind of temptation and the promise of riches could make people do insane things, like try to rob a casino during the middle of an active gang war.

Harvey blinked and wheezed.

Rourke raised his rifle. He was trembling. "Not dead."

Three or four separate bloodstains marked the front of Harvey's button-down shirt, and his left ear had been blown off. Wash of crimson blood down that side of his face. But he was alive, barely breathing. His eyes darted around while his body seemed frozen in that slumped position.

Carter, Rourke, and Micah formed a semi-circle in front of the desk. A Smith & Wesson M&P Shield 9mm sat out of Harvey's reach, and Micah snatched it from him. Stowed the compact gun in his back pocket.

Harvey blinked a few times, then landed on Micah.

"Wait a second," Harvey whispered. "I know you."

"No, you don't."

Harvey's breathing slowed, then left him in one last exhale. His eyes turned glassy and his shoulders rolled forward.

Rourke let out a shuddering sigh. "Carter, open the duffel bag."

Carter had frozen in place, staring at the dead casino owner crumpled in the leather chair.

"Carter," Rourke said. "Duffel."

Carter's head jerked, then he set down his gun and took off his backpack. He opened it and pulled out a duffel bag, which Rourke and Carter started filling with the piles of cash. Some of the stacks were dotted with blood. Micah tried to count as he helped the two of them shove the wrapped stacks of cash into the bag. Half a million, maybe more.

When it was filled, Carter zipped the bag and hefted it over his shoulder. He stumbled a little when the weight of the bag settled on him. "Which way?" he said, then paused as he tried to swallow. He had to tilt his head back to get his throat muscles to work. "Which way do we go?"

Micah eyed the ceiling, and he could still hear gunfire up above. "We can't go out the front. Too much action up there. We exit out through the hockey store, we'll have to fight our way out."

Rourke tilted his head toward the back door. "I say we take our chances going out the back. It's not far to our car. Micah, did you park back there?"

"No, but mine's a rental. Don't worry about that. I'll ride out of here with you guys."

They embarked on their journey to the stairs, but Carter paused to stare at Ethan's body on the floor. "I can't believe we're going to leave him."

Rourke rested a hand on Carter's shoulder. "If we had any other choice, I wouldn't. Come on, Carter, let's get out of here."

Rourke led them back through the casino floor, stepping awkwardly to avoid the jigsaw puzzle of corpses. The fire in the far corner of the room had spread to the nearby wall, and a layer of smoke obscured everything from the waist down. Micah could barely breathe.

Something rustled about thirty feet away, near a coat rack against the wall. Micah barely had time to focus his eyes before a bullet whipped the air, less than a foot from his head. Gangster or cartel member in hiding.

Rourke raised his AK and emptied the magazine, screaming as he did. This only lasted a couple of seconds. The man hiding near the coat rack danced and spun as bullets riddled his body. When the firing stopped, he fell, taking the coat rack with him.

Rourke, panting, shoved a fresh magazine into his rifle. His eyes were bloodshot and panicked. Micah had to move these guys into the outside fresh air, not only because of the billowing smoke, but also before they lost their minds.

Carter shot the dead guy a couple times for good measure. Said nothing, but Micah could hear him whimpering as he readjusted his AK's shoulder strap.

Then they resumed the trek to the back. With each movement closer to that door, Micah considered what they would find out there in the parking lot. The fact that Gustavo had not come barging down the stairs still puzzled him. Micah and the others had been down here for at least five minutes, so it seemed unlikely that the old cartel boss would have waited for so long. Just standing in the lot. Maybe Gustavo hadn't ever spotted him and had pursued Micah because Gustavo had mistaken him for some stray Crossroads mobster.

Micah didn't know. And as they reached the stairs and started to climb, with Rourke in the lead, Carter following, and Micah bringing up the rear, not knowing made him feel like he might puke. He couldn't remember having eaten any breakfast today, but whatever remained in his guts threatened to rise and spray everywhere.

He paused a moment on the third step to gather his thoughts. "Carter. Maybe you should let me go first."

Carter raised two AK-47s, one which had belonged to Ethan. He'd stopped crying, but his eyes were weary and bloodshot. "I'm a little better armed than you. No offense."

"Besides," Rourke said, "I don't hear any gunfire out there. Do you?"

Micah pointed his ear at the closed door above them. He couldn't pinpoint any sounds coming from outside. "No, I guess not."

Carter spun and jogged the last few steps, then he kicked the door open.

# CHAPTER FORTY-THREE

MICAH WATCHED CARTER step out into the humid Flint air outside the Dort Mall. Arms at his sides, the barrels of Carter's twin AK-47s scraping on the concrete. He took three steps onto the pavement, then paused. Tilted his head back and breathed in a lungful.

"Smell that?"

Rourke and Micah stepped into the light, and the door closed behind them.

"What?" Rourke said.

"This whole thing is a massive clusterfuck. I don't even... my best friend is dead, and I don't think... I don't think it's even hit me yet. Don't know how to begin to process something like that. But that smell? That's the scent of justice. Of us being rich as fuck. I know that Ethan would have—"

Carter's words were lost underneath the blast of a

pistol. The bullet punctured his chest and he stumbled forward, then fell flat on his face. His bag slumped to his side. The pistol shot echoed from the mall exterior to the trees lining the edge of the lot.

"What is in the bag?" said a familiar voice from behind.

Gustavo Salazar.

Rourke spun, but before he could raise his rifle, another gunshot rang out and he clutched his side. He staggered back, collapsing against the building. Still alive, at least for now. Bullet wound in his stomach.

Micah raised his hands, the Glock in his right. Finger off the trigger.

Gustavo had been hiding behind the door and currently had a gun trained. He'd patiently waited out here for Micah to return from inside the casino. Ten minutes, standing there against the mall exterior, waiting, anticipating.

There was no point trying to run. Gus' trigger finger was quicker than Micah's legs.

"Weapons on the ground," Gustavo said.

Micah tossed his pistol out in front of him. He tried to aim it far enough away to satisfy Gustavo, but maybe close enough that he could somersault and grab it. That was a long shot, but he might have no other choice.

Rourke hesitated, and then Gustavo circled around them. He had a Desert Eagle in each hand. One pointed at Rourke, one at Micah.

"Drop that rifle right now. If you don't, I will shoot you where you stand. I am faster than you, I guarantee it."

Rourke shrugged his shoulder to loosen the strap, then he let the AK-47 slip from his fingers. He clasped both hands to his side. He was pressed up against the wall, his breathing shallow and erratic. Blood leaking out from between his fingers.

"Do you have another in an ankle holster?" Gustavo asked Micah.

He shook his head.

Gustavo came to a stop, now facing the two of them. Micah wondered where Gustavo's other men had gone. Maybe he'd dismissed them to handle Micah on his own.

Yes, he would want that pleasure all to himself.

"Michael. It has been a long time, hasn't it?"

"I go by Micah now."

Gustavo sniffed. "You changed your name? I am not surprised. No wonder we have had such trouble finding you."

"You didn't find me. I came to you."

"Yes, you did, didn't you? When they approached us about that body in the morgue they said was you, I did not believe it from the start. We sent someone to look, but that was more of a..." he waved one of the Desert Eagles in a circle, searching for the right word. "Exercise. I always had a feeling you were not dead, even before that. All those rumors. I always held out hope I would see you again, in the flesh. Prayed I would get the chance to confront the traitor."

"And now here I am."

"Here you are. Tell me: what is in the duffel bag?"

"The casino's money," Micah said.

"Damn it, Micah, don't tell him shit," Rourke said, his voice raspy. "We're not giving him a cent of it."

Gustavo smiled. "Your friend thinks he has a choice here about the money. This makes me laugh."

Micah peeked at the AK-47 on the ground, halfway between him and Rourke. It was closer than the Glock he'd jettisoned.

Gustavo's fingers were on the triggers, though. He wouldn't have time. And if Micah attempted anything, Gustavo would know instantly.

"How come you're the only one here?" Micah said.

"I want to show them your dead body, not tell them. It will be more dramatic."

Only Gustavo had seen Micah. That gave him a tiny amount of hope, at least. And it made sense. If they'd all spotted him, he'd be facing a firing squad right now.

On the other side of the mall, the rabble of gunfire had died down in the last few seconds. A moment of silence thundered all around them. Then, a chorus of police sirens chirped, and a new round of weapons blasting began.

"Cops are coming," Micah said.

"I am not concerned," Gustavo said with a grin. "You won't live to see them arrive. They will not be coming to your rescue this time."

Micah wondered if he could keep Gustavo distracted long enough for the cops to circle around the back and find them. And, if upon seeing police cars, Gus would empty his clip into Micah's head before dashing into the trees.

"Tell me this," Gustavo said. "What went wrong with you, Michael? How could you have turned on our family? How could you have talked to the federal government and put so many of our brothers and sisters in prison? I have always wanted to understand what possessed you to do such a thing."

Out of the corner of his eye, Micah caught Rourke frowning.

Rourke had to be working on a plan to get to that AK. Or, maybe he had another gun stashed on him somewhere. Either way, he was too injured to move quickly, and maybe he knew that. Maybe he realized that if he tried something, Gustavo only had to flick his finger to kill him.

"Tell me," Gustavo said.

Micah shook his head. Wouldn't give the bastard the satisfaction.

Gustavo lowered one of the Desert Eagles to point it at Micah's knee. "Then this is what we will do. You will die today, no matter what, because of your recent treachery. But, because of your loyalty before that, I will give you a choice. You can tell me everything that happened, and I will shoot you in the head. Or, you can stay silent, and I will start with your knees, and the end will only get worse from there."

"What the hell is going on here?" Rourke said. The other two ignored him.

Micah's stomach churned. His eyes blurred. He could

tell his hands were shaking, and the last thing he wanted was for Gustavo to see how afraid he was. Micah had always suspected that the cartel would someday catch up with him. By coming to Michigan, he had delivered himself to them, wrapped in a bow.

"I gave you a choice, Michael. Are you deciding?"

In a flash, Micah understood everything Frank had been trying to teach him about powerlessness. Micah had been unable to accept the conditions and events in the world he could not change. He had no control over this situation, and his crime had been thinking he could fix all of this.

The sudden understanding filled him with a distinct buoyancy as if he'd heaved a lungful of air and grown an inch taller. Too bad he'd be dead long before he could appreciate this new enlightenment.

"I need your answer," Gustavo said.

Micah gritted his teeth. More sirens chirped, now coming closer.

Gustavo sighed. "Sounds like we won't be able to play anymore. Get on your knees."

Time to die.

But then, he remembered Harvey's pistol, stashed in his back pocket.

Micah's knees bent, and he slowly sank to the ground while lowering his hands. His eyes stayed on Gustavo as he moved, and Gus apparently didn't notice that his hands were nearing his waist. Gustavo's smug grin told Micah where his attention was.

So as his hands were at the same level as his waistband, Micah snatched the 9mm pistol from his back pocket. Whipped it forward. Finger wrapped around the trigger.

Gus' eyes jumped wide, but he didn't have enough time to react.

Micah shot him in the stomach. Gus pulled his trigger, but the bullet went over Micah's left shoulder. Micah heard it blast away a chunk of the Dort Mall.

He had just enough time to see the look of shock on Gustavo's face before Micah squeezed the trigger three more times, hitting his target twice in the chest and once in the shoulder.

His old boss twisted and fell to the ground. Micah leaped forward and kicked the guns away from him. Gustavo's eyes darted back and forth as his hands flailed, trying to search the ground around him for his pistol.

"Your guns are gone," Micah said.

Gustavo's chest seized. His breath wheezed out one last time as his eyes fluttered and his head lolled to the side.

"You okay?" Micah asked Rourke.

Rourke staggered to his feet. "I'm shot. That son of a bitch shot me."

The echoing blue and red lights came from around the corner of the mall. The nose of a car poked out, and Micah's pulse skyrocketed.

"We have to go, now," Micah said as he shoved the pistol in his waistband. He snatched the Glock off the ground and scurried over to Rourke.

Rourke lurched forward, bent, grabbed the duffel bag,

and grunted as he hoisted it from the ground. "Sorry, Carter," he muttered. "You deserved better than this."

Since Rourke was distracted by the heap of flesh on the ground that used to be his friend, Micah grabbed him by the shirt sleeve and dragged him off toward the trees.

# CHAPTER FORTY-FOUR

MICAH SNEAKED ONE last glance at the bodies of Carter and Gustavo as he helped Rourke across the parking lot and into the trees past the edge. Rourke dragged the duffel bag behind him by the strap, with his other hand squeezing his stomach. The duffel's zipper scraped along the concrete. Blood dribbled over Rourke's hand as he ran.

"Where's your car? You have one here, right?" Micah said.

Rourke grunted. "Just on the other side of these trees."

The revolving blue and white lights bounced off the exterior of the mall, then faded as the two thieves disappeared into the trees. Micah glanced back to see one of the cars stop a few feet from the dead bodies by the back door.

Two cops jumped out of the car, weapons drawn. Shouting at the dead people to put their hands on their heads. One of the cops squatted next to Gustavo and felt for a pulse.

"Wait, wait," Rourke said.

Micah let go of his arm and Rourke backed into a tree, then closed his eyes. "I just need a second."

The duffel fell out of Rourke's bloody grip. He tried to grab it, but his hands were too slippery. He was in bad shape, and would bleed out in a few minutes if he didn't get to a hospital.

"We have to leave," Micah said. "They're going to come back to these woods, too."

Rourke ignored him. "I can't believe they're dead. Twenty minutes ago, they were alive. Now, they're not. It's me. I did this. I did all of this and now…"

Micah recognized that look of consciousness on Rourke's face. The adrenaline was wearing off, and he was becoming aware of the consequences. Understanding what he'd lost.

"I'm sorry about your friends, Rourke. There was no way a robbery like this was going to go smoothly. You're lucky any of you made it out alive."

"I knew this might happen, but still…"

Micah knew what he meant, and a pang of memory burned at him. "Yeah, it doesn't make it any easier, knowing that. I've lost friends before, too."

Rourke looked up, meeting Micah's eyes for the first time since they made it out. "What did that guy mean back there, about you turning on your family and something about the feds? Why did he call you Michael?"

Micah hesitated because too many people knew his secret. But Rourke knew enough already that he could probably guess the rest. If he lived, anyway. That hole in his side wasn't going to close itself.

"I was a member of the Sinaloa cartel, a few years ago. The feds caught up with me, and I had some pretty serious charges on my head. So I chose to snitch instead of spending my life in prison."

"So this crew Crossroads was fighting against, they're your people?"

Micah shook his head. "Not anymore."

"Because you're in Witness Protection?"

"I was. Dropped out not too long ago. If you don't have any more questions, can we please go now? Give me your keys and I'll drive."

Rourke moaned as he dug his bloody hand into his pocket to fish out the keys. He tossed them to Micah. Micah barely caught the slippery things. Rourke nodded a few hundred yards to the right, at a car parked in a small clearing in the woods.

Micah helped him stumble through the trees, duffel bag trailing behind. The damn thing weighed a ton, and as Micah's adrenaline was also waning, his body begged him to take a break. His muscles felt like taffy stretched to the breaking point.

Once at the car, Micah helped Rourke get in and then he slid into the driver's seat.

Rourke hefted the bag onto his knees and unzipped it. "I don't know if it's fair for me to give you half. I think maybe Ethan and Carter's families should get their share. Maybe. I can't think straight right now."

Micah stared at the unzipped bag, at the green stacks bubbling up to the top of the opening. He could do a lot with that money. Money stolen from a white supremacist gangster, who had himself pilfered it from others. Maybe not stolen, exactly. They'd lost it gambling in his casino, or had bought heroin or crack from him, or spent it on Harvey's whores.

"I don't want a share," Micah said. "Give your friends' families their share."

Rourke looked puzzled for a second, then he slowly nodded. "Where are we going?"

Micah started the car. "Hospital."

He piloted the car out of the clearing and onto a dirt path with tall trees lining the sides. This path connected with a park, then the main road. He joined it, found no cops in the immediate vicinity. Still, he drove swiftly but not erratically. They were so close, couldn't make any mistakes now.

Rourke groaned and pressed on his bloody stomach. "What's it like to be in Witness Protection?"

"Lonely."

# CHAPTER FORTY-FIVE

MICAH BUZZED THE door outside the third floor of the hospital, waiting for someone to let him in. An old-style coiled phone hanging on the wall chirped.

Micah picked it up. "Hello?"

"Can I help you?" said a woman's distorted voice.

"I'm here to see Frank Mueller. His room is... 315. I think."

"Are you family, sir?"

"More or less. He's my boss."

The woman hesitated, sighed, then the door clicked and cracked open a fraction of an inch. Micah pushed through, then poked around for the room signs. When he found 315, he yanked the heavy door to find Frank in a hospital bed. He was awake and smiling. A woman was sitting in a chair, her back to Micah.

"Hey, kid," Frank said.

The woman turned. Frank's sister Anita. Her broad grin and brilliant white teeth lifted Micah's heart. He gave his best effort to mirror her smile.

"As I live and breathe. Micah Reed. How are you, dear?"

Micah crossed the room and leaned in to kiss Anita on the cheek. He sneaked a glance at Frank, in the bed. The old man looked weary but alert.

"It's good to see you, Anita."

"Did everything turn out okay?"

Micah nodded. "Basically. Maybe it's better if you don't know all the details."

"I understand."

"How is DC these days?"

She batted a hand. "Oh, you know. The people without the power will do anything to get it, and the people with the power will do anything to keep it. The names on the offices change but everything else stays the same."

"The cycle of life," Micah said, and Anita giggled. She was a bit of a flirty old woman.

"Anita," Frank said, "do you think you might give Micah and me a minute?"

She looked back and forth between them, then quietly got up to leave the room. She paused in front of Micah, put a hand on his arm.

"I know you don't want to give me details, but was it a productive visit? Are things better now than they were before?"

Micah shrugged. "It's hard to say."

She smiled knowingly, even though there was no way

she could understand what Micah had learned. She gave him a peck on the cheek and she waddled out of the room.

Once she was gone, Frank motioned to the now-empty chair.

"You were right," Micah said.

Frank chuckled. "You're going to have to be more specific. I'm right a lot."

"About powerlessness. The first step."

Frank swished his lips back and forth, considering. "It's not an easy lesson to digest. It's even less fun to learn because it usually comes with some kind of hardship. Growth comes from pain, is what my friend Red Sweater Barry used to say about it."

"You feeling okay?" Micah said.

"I'm good. Not much pain. They cut out a part of me that I don't need, and I don't miss it. I've mostly been sitting here, wondering why the hell God put that in me in the first place, if it was only going to make me feel like my guts were being ripped out, all this time later."

"Who knows?"

"Anyway," Frank said. "Aside from some residual smoker's lung damage, they gave me a clean bill of health. I get out tomorrow."

"Good."

"Enough about that. Tell me what happened today. I wasn't sure if I was ever going to see you again, after that last phone call. You just had to go dashing off like a damn knight, trying to save everyone."

Micah opened his mouth, but he didn't know where to

start. His lip trembled, and a wetness came to the corners of his eyes. "Logan King's mother Yvette. They came for her, and I tried to stop it. I wasn't quick enough."

Frank frowned, then handed Micah a tissue from the box next to his bed. "I'm sorry, kid. I'm sure you did what you could, but if she was mixed up with them, her days were numbered. They would have gotten her eventually."

Micah dabbed his eyes with the tissue. "Maybe so."

"Tell me what happened at the casino."

Micah pulled in a lungful of air to compose himself. He figured he should stick to the high points. "You were right. You were right the whole time. The cartel figured out the Crossroads gang was trying to fool them, and instead raided the casino. There was a big gunfight at the standoff. Everyone's dead."

Frank narrowed his eyes, lingering over his thoughts for a few seconds. "You're not dead."

"Not as far as I know."

Frank grinned. "The rental car?"

"Sorry, Frank. It's toast. Took quite a few rounds from the cartel when I arrived at the mall."

"Hmm. Would have been better *not* to have it all shot up to hell, but I'll figure something out. You didn't get shot, and that's what matters."

Micah eased closer in the chair. "Did we do something good here? I need to know that everything we and everyone else went through wasn't pointless. Did we help?"

Frank shrugged, then grimaced a bit at the movement. "Who can say? We made it out alive, with most of our parts intact. That's what matters, I think. Sometimes, that's the best you can hope for."

"I saw one of my old cartel bosses. He cornered me and I shot him four times."

Frank winced. "I'm sorry you had to do that. But with these people, it's either them or you. Like I said, we're still alive."

"What do we do now?"

Frank shrugged, then groaned a little and put a hand on his side. "We go back to Denver and we meet up at the office on Monday. We find some new bail cases to work and get back into our groove."

The prospect of returning to his day job gave Micah a bit of calm. He wanted to be home. To return to the normalcy of regular life.

Frank opened his mouth to speak, but then his head jerked a fraction of an inch. "Wait a second. Did you say Logan's mother was named Yvette?"

"Yes."

"Yvette King?"

Micah nodded.

Frank tilted his head at the wall to his left. "I think you should check 321. Three rooms down on this side."

"What's going on?"

"Just go look. I'll be here when you get back."

Micah stood, thoroughly confused. He backed out of the room, maintaining eye contact with Frank until he had to pivot to find the door. Outside of the room, Anita was sitting in a chair against the wall, smiling her warm smile at him. Aging paperback in her hands.

Micah turned left and passed 317 and 319, then paused in front of 321. A chart hanging from the wall outside read *Yvette King.* A few lines down, it mentioned *throat lacerations.* She'd arrived on the helicopter.

"Excuse me?" said a voice from behind. Thick accent, something Creole.

Micah turned to find a portly nurse in camouflage scrubs. Arms crossed.

"Can I help you?"

"I'm just going in to visit Yvette."

The woman pursed her lips. "She only got out of surgery a few minutes ago, and now she's resting. Are you family?"

"Yes," Micah said, without hesitation. "I'm her son."

The nurse eyed him, clucked her teeth a couple times, then nodded at the door. "Go ahead then, child. But be quick about it. Quick, like a bunny."

He thanked her and opened the door. In a bed, hooked to beeping machines and with an IV bag hovering above her, Yvette King was sleeping. Bandaged from her chin to her collarbone. Last time he'd seen her, he was positive she'd died after Bushy Eyebrows had slashed her throat.

A neighbor must have heard the gunshots and called the police, who called an ambulance. Then the helicopter brought her here. There was no other reasonable explanation.

Micah tiptoed into the room and slid into the chair

next to her bed. He watched the rise and fall of her chest, the fluttering of her eyelids as she dreamed. One of her hands was above the blanket.

Micah took her hand and laced his fingers through hers.

∾

If you enjoyed this book, please click here to leave a review.

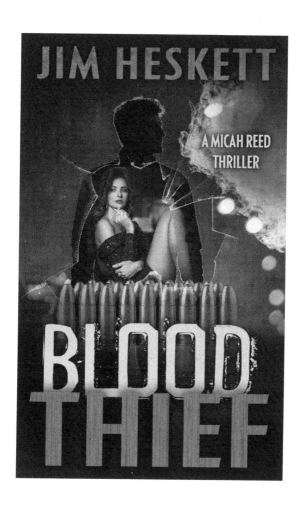

Ready for more? Get the sequel BLOOD THIEF at
www.jimheskett.com/blood

## NOTE TO READERS

Ready to get the next book in the series? Visit
www.jimheskett.com/blood

Also, join my reader group at www.jimheskett.com to get
updates and free stuff!

If you started reading Micah Reed's adventure with this
book, go back and take a gander at Airbag Scars. Micah's
backstory will make a lot more sense.

With that out of the way, thank you for reading my book!

Having married into a Michigan family, I've spent quit a
bit of time up there in the area "under the bridge." There is
a real mall in Flint I used as inspiration for the setting for
this book. My wife is friends with the mall owner, so I've
been able to see back rooms in the mall not many people

have access to. There's no hidden casino in the basement, though (as far as I know).

In this book, we get to know Micah's sage Obi-Wan mentor Frank better, and we see bits and pieces of Micah's past. Also, remember the strip club owner Tyson Darby, from early in the book? Stay tuned, you'll see him again later on down the line...

Please consider leaving reviews on Goodreads and wherever else you purchased the book (links to retailers at www.jimheskett.com/casino). You have no idea how much it will help the success of this book and my ability to write future books. That, sharing it on social media, and telling other people to read it.

Are you interested in joining a community of Jim Heskett fiction fans? Discuss the books with other people, including the author! Join for free at www.jimheskett.com/bookophile

I have a website where you can learn more about me and my other projects. Check me out at www.jimheskett.com and sign up for my reader group so you can stay informed on the latest news. You'll even get some freebies for signing up. You like free stuff, right?

*For Lisa, Don and Kay, Lahna and Kevin, Tiff and Tony. Cold lakes and a wet mitten.*

Published by Royal Arch Books

Www.RoyalArchBooks.com

Please consider leaving a review once you have finished this book. Want to know when the next book is coming out? Join my mailing list to get updates and free stuff!

For a full list of all Jim Heskett's books, please visit
www.RoyalArchBooks.com

If you like thrillers, you'll want to take a gander at my
Whistleblower Trilogy. The first book, Wounded Animals,
follows the story of Tucker Candle, who meets a mysterious
stranger who warns him not to take a business trip. Candle goes,
however, and when he comes home, he discovers a dead man in
his bathroom and his wife is missing.

# ABOUT THE AUTHOR

Jim Heskett was born in the wilds of Oklahoma, raised by a pack of wolves with a station wagon and a membership card to the local public swimming pool. Just like the man in the John Denver song, he moved to Colorado in the summer of his 27th year, and never looked back. Aside from an extended break traveling the world, he hasn't let the Flatirons mountains out of his sight.

He fell in love with writing at the age of fourteen with a copy of Stephen King's The Shining. Poetry became his first outlet for teen angst, then later some terrible screenplays, and eventually short and long fiction. In between, he worked a few careers that never quite tickled his creative toes, and hasn't ever forgotten about Stephen King. You can find him currently huddled over a laptop in an undisclosed location in Colorado, dreaming up ways to kill beloved characters.

He blogs at his own site and hosts the Indie Author Answers Podcast. You can also scour the internet to find the occasional guest post or podcast appearance. A curated list of media appearances can be found at www.jimheskett.com/media

He believes the huckleberry is the king of berries and refuses to be persuaded in any other direction.

If you'd like to ask a question or just to say hi, stop by the About page and fill out the contact form.

*More Info:*
www.jimheskett.com

39605673R00185

Made in the USA
Lexington, KY
20 May 2019